Girl
ON THE
Run

Also by Abigail Johnson

If I Fix You

The First to Know

Even if I Fall

Every Other Weekend

Girl on the Run

ABIGAIL JOHNSON

Underlined

Text copyright © 2020 by Abigail Johnson
Cover photograph (girl) copyright © 2020 by Boris Jovanovic/Stocksy;
(background) copyright © 2020 by Robert Jones/Arcangel
Cover design by kid-ethic

Visit us on the Web! GetUnderlined.com

Educators and librarians, for a variety of teaching tools, visit us at
RHTeachersLibrarians.com

Library of Congress Cataloging-in-Publication Data
Names: Johnson, Abigail, author.
Title: Girl on the run / Abigail Johnson.
Description: First edition. | New York : Underlined, [2020] | Audience: Ages 12 and up. |
Summary: Sixteen-year-old Katelyn, who has been subjected to her mother's "wanderlust"
all her life, discovers that Mom might not be who she says she is, and that someone is
hunting them both.
Identifiers: LCCN 2020003757 (print) | LCCN 2020003758 (ebook) |
ISBN 978-0-593-17981-9 (trade paperback) | ISBN 978-0-593-17982-6 (ebook)
Subjects: CYAC: Mothers and daughters—Fiction. | Secrets—Fiction. | Mystery and
detective stories.
Classification: LCC PZ7.1.J59 Gir 2020 (print) | LCC PZ7.1.J59 (ebook) | DDC [Fic]—dc

The text of this book is set in 11.2-point Warnock Pro Light.
Interior design by Cathy Bobak

Printed in the United States of America
10 9 8 7 6 5 4 3 2 1
First Edition

For Rory
You were the sweetest baby and the kindest kid,
and I know you're going to be the most amazing man.

FOUND

Aiden isn't watching the movie.

My skin grows warm as I realize he's not even pretending to watch the movie.

"You know, you were the one who picked this." I extend a finger toward my laptop. "What happened to all that 'I can't believe you've lived in New Jersey for nearly a year and you still haven't seen *Garden State*'?"

I barely get the words out before Aiden's hand fits to my jaw and he leans in to kiss me. It's a good kiss, the kind that makes my skin tingle and the whole world fade away until we're the only two people on the planet. His free hand slides around my waist, pulling me closer, and a light sigh escapes from me. I could get so lost in him if I let myself.

That thought abruptly brings reality back into focus, and I shimmy from Aiden's arms until we're awkwardly sitting beside each other again in the reading chair that's meant for only

1

one person. This chair, my bed, and my thrift-shop desk and dresser make up the entirety of the furniture in my room—unless you count the boxes I never bothered to unpack.

Easygoing almost to a fault, Aiden lets me go without protest, raising a single eyebrow. "Did you hear your mom or something?"

I shake my head and shift to the cushioned armrest so we're no longer smooshed together. "She left barely an hour ago. That would be a new record for world's shortest first date, even for her." I want to check the window, though, and he knows it.

Aiden toys with a thread from the frayed knee of my jeans. There's an ease to the way he's touching me that screams boyfriend. I shiver involuntarily, which in turn makes me inch my leg away.

"Would it be so horrible if she knew about me?" he says. "I mean, we've technically already met." He glances over at the hiking boots next to my dresser, the ones he sold me and Mom four months ago, before she and I hiked the Smoky Mountains over the summer. I'd wanted to go to Disneyland, but she gets superanxious in big crowds, so she surprised me with a road trip and a secluded weeklong hike instead, which, I'll admit now, turned out kind of amazing. So did the cute REI sales associate who oh so casually slipped me his number while Mom was checking out mini stoves.

I gnaw my lip, trying to think of a way to say that, yes, it would be horrible if Mom knew about him, without actually having to say yes. I settle on "It's not you."

In response, Aiden slowly nods. "Right."

"It's not." I reach for the hand he's drawn back. "It's not even her. It's me."

He gives me a humorless smile. "Ashamed of me, huh? No, I get it. Guys who volunteer at animal shelters are generally dicks."

"No." I let my mouth curve up. "But they do sometimes smell like cat pee."

A genuine laugh erupts from Aiden. "Seriously? I try to be really careful about that."

I lean forward to brush his cheek with a kiss, catching a hint of something crisp and foresty and definitely not at all like cat pee. When I start to stand, Aiden tugs me back.

"Then what?" His voice is as gentle as his touch. "'Cause I keep expecting you to just ghost me one of these days, and I'm fully ready to admit how much that would suck." His hand slips over mine. "I like you, Katelyn. I'm fine if it's more than you like me, but tell me I'm not wasting my time here."

Every bit of the humor that initially attracted me to Aiden is gone. We've always kept things light and fun. Now he looks like my next words have all the power in the world to elate or crush him.

And I will crush him. Not intentionally, and probably not without crushing myself a bit in the process, but it's going to happen. Not because Aiden is a bad guy—I think the fact that he's in my bedroom despite all Mom's rules speaks for itself. As does the fact that he made a cute Rapunzel joke instead of complaining when I told him he'd have to climb the drainpipe and sneak into my bedroom if he wanted to see me. I couldn't risk letting him use the front entrance like a normal person (I wouldn't put it past Mom to rig the door with some kind of undetectable sign to check if it's been opened when she leaves me home alone).

I should probably explain about my mom.

She's amazing and funny—but nearly every hour of the day she's terrified out of her mind that something terrible is going to happen to me. I think it has to do with how she grew up. She's never been exactly forthcoming about her past, but I do know that her mom dropped her on the doorstep of her unsuspecting father's trailer when she was three, never to be seen again, and that the height of her dad's parenting skills was remembering to feed her most of the time. He died shortly before I was born, so I never met him, but given my mom's lack of parental supervision growing up, it seems like she swung really far the other way with me.

Until a few years ago, the only time I was allowed on the computer was for school—home school, that is. And I think it was more my mom's fear of algebra than any of my pleading that finally made her relent and allow me to go to public school. Though, to be fair, it might also have been the hunger strike I enacted.

It took me a little longer to convince her to let me get a cell phone, which I finally accomplished by printing out news stories at school about kids who got kidnapped and saved themselves by calling for help. Were some of them stories I wrote myself using mock-up layouts I found online? Maybe. But sometimes my mom needs that extra push to rein in the superparanoid would-keep-me-in-a-bubble-forever mentality that defines her as a parent.

I've learned that the best way to get what I want is to either convince her I'm in more danger if she doesn't listen to my suggestions (e.g., public school, a cell phone) or just keep a few harmless details from her (e.g., Aiden).

Most days, I think she knows I cut corners when it comes to her rules, but I like to think she's the teeniest bit proud of me when I figure out how to get around one. I'm not stupid enough to flaunt Aiden in front of her, though, which is why I practically shove him off the chair when I hear the front door open downstairs.

She did break her record. It isn't even nine o'clock yet.

"Katelyn?"

"In my room!" I call, jumping up and pushing Aiden toward the window.

"Is this my answer?" There's a teasing quality to his voice that I can appreciate only because he has the good sense to whisper.

"Know what happened to the last guy my mom found in my room?"

"He got invited to dinner?"

5

"He got a face full of pepper spray." All because he was trying to decorate my room to invite me to a dance. Poor guy. And poor me, since Mom and I ended up moving right after—Mom says the two are unrelated, but I doubt it.

She calls it wanderlust, but I'm not sure that's what it is. She'll be fine one day, and the next I'll come home from school to find that she's quit her job and already has half our belongings in boxes—hence the unpacked ones stacked in my room. We're closing in on a year in our current duplex, and I'm hoping to make it through graduation here, if nothing else. But that means getting Mom to make some ties in Bridgeton so she won't want to leave the next time she gets an itch.

My greatest triumph of the past year was getting her to agree to start dating, something she hasn't done since my dad died, despite the frequent offers she gets. She had me when she was only nineteen, so she's still young and looks amazing—also thanks to the fact that we run together every morning. She has stunning green eyes and thick auburn hair that reaches halfway down her back. My eyes and hair are the same color as hers but not nearly as striking. The main difference between us is that my skin is more olive than her fair, sunburn-prone complexion, a gift from a man I barely remember.

Based on the way she still tears up on the rare occasions I get her to talk about my dad, I'm not expecting her to fall madly in love with one of the guys she dates, but a little flirting and fun would be good for her. And any reason to stay in one place long enough for it to feel like home is good enough for me.

If she found Aiden in my room, she'd have a moving truck in our driveway before he even made it out the window.

I push him again. "You have to go."

"Meet me tomorrow."

"I—" I start to object, since I have no idea how I'll slip away from Mom, but he looks perfectly content—eager, even—to get caught. "Fine."

"Promise?"

I almost grit my teeth, but I remember that he's still waiting for my answer about whether he's wasting his time with me. I know what I want the answer to be, but hearing Mom's footsteps on the stairs, I give Aiden one last shove. "I promise." He climbs out the window, only to dart back in the second I start to turn away—to kiss me one more time.

"Go!" I hiss, trying not to smile. I don't breathe again until he clears the frame so I can close the window and yank the curtain shut.

By the time Mom enters my room, I'm sitting at my desk, laptop open and an acceptably academic website on the screen, with my history book beside me.

"Oh, hey, one sec," I say, turning my head but keeping my eyes glued to the page, because if I'm gonna play the dedicated student, I'm gonna sell it. At last, I sigh triumphantly, as though finishing the section I was reading, and twist in my seat to face her, propping my chin in my hands on the backrest and grinning. "So is my new dad waiting downstairs?"

Mom shudders in response. "I pray to God that man never procreates." Then she frowns at me. "Honey, are you feeling okay? Your skin's all flushed." When she reaches to brush my hair away for a closer look, I pull back and try not to look too guilty as my face blazes with anxiety and embarrassment. I put a few feet between us by casually moving to sit in the middle of my bed.

"I'm fine. Don't change the subject. Aren't you being a bit dramatic? You spent less than two hours with the guy. What was wrong with this one?"

"Besides the fact that he kept staring down our waitress's blouse every time she refilled our drinks?"

"Ew, really?" My shoulders relax, now that she's no longer scrutinizing my appearance.

"And then he didn't even tip her."

I scrunch up my face to an almost painful degree. There is a special circle in hell for nontippers. Another huge concession on Mom's part this year was letting me get an after-school waitressing job, so I know from experience. Mom's date could have started picking his nose at the table, and I'd still say his cheapness was his biggest character flaw.

She leans one hand on my bed so she can take off her heels. "Can we just agree now that trying to date after thirty-five is evil and I can give it up?"

"If something is hard, quit right away. Got it."

Mom flops back and starts the contortionist act required to free herself from her Spanx. "What if I just got like a dozen cats instead?"

"Mom."

"And I could start eating frosting right out of the can. You know I've always wanted to do that."

"Then I will drop out of school and start auditioning for reality TV shows. Mom, I will go on *The Bachelor*. I'll do it."

Freed from her Spanx, Mom folds them neatly in her lap. "It's just so demoralizing."

I'm not sure if she's talking about her dating failures or *The Bachelor*. Probably both. "We just need to widen the net a little." I'm more confident than ever in the surprise I've been working on.

"Okay, so don't get mad," I say, leaping up. "Even though I'm the one with the birthday next week, I got *you* a present. I know you don't want me posting anything about myself online, because you watch way too much *Dateline*." I tug her to sit in my desk chair. "And I didn't," I add quickly when she pales. "But you are an adult, and I thought you might . . . have . . . better . . . success . . ." I slow my words as I lean over her, fingers flying across the keys to pull up the site I'm looking for. "I knew it! Look, a half dozen messages already." I point at the tiny counter on the screen and wait for the panicky, wide-eyed look to leave her face.

It doesn't.

Her voice drops low as she reaches for the laptop. "Katelyn, what did you do?"

"It's a completely nonscuzzy dating site for 'mature adults looking for lasting relationships,'" I say, reciting the website's slogan. "I created a profile for you, and there are plenty of guys interested, even with your nearly seventeen-year-old kid and all. Look, I even included a photo of us from the day we moved in."

"When?" She shoots a hand out to wrap almost painfully around my wrist.

"I did it after you left for your date. I thought you'd . . . I'm sorry. I'll take it down." She's overreacting. Again. It's not like I passed out copies of her social security card. I was just trying to help her go on a date that didn't end with us splitting a carton of cookie-dough ice cream and watching a Jason Statham movie.

It takes me less than a minute to delete her profile, but the second I'm done, Mom slams the laptop shut and pulls her phone from her purse, calling a number without hesitation.

"It's me," she says, in a voice so calm it makes the hair on my arms stand up. "There may be a problem. I need to know—" Her hand clenches tighter around the phone. "How long?"

She's moving even before she hangs up, throwing my closet door open and grabbing an old backpack that I keep meaning to get rid of. Then she's at my dresser, pulling drawers out and stuffing random fistfuls of clothes into the bag.

"What are you doing?"

"We have to go." She doesn't bother to close the drawers once she empties them. That carelessness from someone who irons my socks on a regular basis is more unsettling than her words. I don't move. "Katelyn, now!" She crosses to the desk and yanks me away with such force that I nearly topple to the floor. My history book thuds as it hits the ground, and Mom's grip tightens at the sound.

"Mom, stop! We're not moving because I made you a dating profile. It's gone, deleted. I know you get freaked out by stuff like this." I raise my eyebrows and add, mostly to myself, "But you're scaring me." My heart beats painfully in my chest. I'm about to offer to go buy hot butterscotch for the ice cream and to suggest she take a bath, but she's not calming down or showing even a hint of embarrassment over her behavior. If anything, she squeezes my arm tighter.

"What is going on?" I say.

She raises her eyes to mine and holds my gaze for several beats, a few seconds maybe, but it's enough to give weight to her words. She releases my arm. "They found us."

RUN

"Who found us? Who was that on the phone?" I stand completely still in the center of my room, but my blood is racing like I just ran a marathon. Mom is cautious to a fault, and I'm used to her worrying over little things, going so far as to randomly pick me up in the middle of a sleepover or to install tracking software on my phone. Once she even made me "break up" with my best friend when she found out her mom was a cop and kept a gun in the house. Never mind that they had a gun safe, which my friend didn't even know the location of, much less the code to.

But this . . . She isn't panicked. She doesn't look scared. She looks scary.

"Grab only what you need from the bathroom. I'll explain once we're in the car." The thing that keeps me from asking more questions is the sheen of sweat on her forehead, along with the quick, methodical movements she makes as she circles my room, grabbing essentials until my bag is full.

12

Mom's paranoia is not new to me, but we've been doing so well lately, and even at her worst, she's never dragged me out of the house with such hastily packed bags before. Granted, I've always followed her strict internet rules until now—well, mostly—but all this because of a dating profile?

It makes no sense. She speaks again when I fail to adopt her urgency. "Right now. You need to trust me."

And I do. I don't know what's going on or why she's having the mother of all freak-outs, but I know something is wrong and that she's doing what she thinks she has to do to keep us safe.

And for now, that's enough.

I slide past her into my bathroom, grabbing only what I need—but for what? How can I possibly pack for a trip I don't know anything about? Mom's breathing is rapid as she darts down the hall to her room. I catch a glimpse of her face, hard and determined . . . but not surprised. Almost as though she's been waiting for this.

I stop hesitating after that. I sweep a hand through the bottom shelf in my medicine cabinet, knocking the contents into a toiletry bag. I get back to my bedroom just as she does. She's changed into jeans and a dark T-shirt and is carrying her own bag now. She rushes me down the hall, down the stairs, and through the kitchen, flipping every light switch on and detouring into the living room to turn on the TV and crank up the volume. I watch her like she's a stranger.

Then we're gone, not out the front door, but the back,

running barefoot through the yard, right up to our neighbor's seven-foot-high wooden fence. Mom tosses our shoes and our bags to the other side, then bends and laces her fingers together.

"I'll boost you." Every gesture speaks of urgency.

I place my foot into her hands, and her strength in launching me off the ground draws a gasp from my lips. Mom is five foot nothing and weighs a buck ten soaking wet. Her sudden strength makes my blood race even faster.

The slats dig painfully into my stomach until I get both legs over the top and jump down. My palms hit damp grass, and before I can turn back and wonder how Mom is going to scale the fence without help, she lands next to me.

"Mom," I say, impressed despite the panic nipping at my heels. She ignores me and grabs my hand, just as I've tugged my shoes on. We race through another yard, around the side of that house, and then stop. Mom starts up the walkway to Mr. Guillory's front door.

"Do not say a word," she tells me, setting our bags out of sight and slapping a bright smile on her face. She rings the bell.

Mr. Guillory is well into his seventies, with a generous paunch and a full head of silvery-white hair, which stands in sharp contrast with his dark skin. Even at this hour, he greets us with his usual friendly smile as he opens his door.

"Well, hello there, Melissa, Katelyn. What can I do for you on this lovely Friday night?"

"Actually, we're a little embarrassed," Mom says, looking

indeed as if that were the case. "We're having a girls' night junk-food fest, and we decided"—she puts an arm around my shoulder and taps her head with mine—"that we couldn't rest until we ate our weight in snickerdoodles. Would you be willing to spare a cup of sugar? We'd be glad to share some of the cookies with you."

Mr. Guillory is only too happy to gift us with as much sugar as we want. We follow him into his kitchen—or, rather, I follow him. Mom disappears somewhere after the entryway. Before I can wonder if I'm still supposed to keep silent, she reappears. Mr. Guillory straightens up after retrieving a nearly full bag of sugar from one of his lower cabinets.

"Perfect." Mom snatches the bag from him a little too quickly. "We'll bring the cookies over tomorrow."

As soon as Mr. Guillory sees us to the door and closes it behind us, Mom retrieves our bags, grabs my arm, and hurries me onto the dimly lit street. She dumps the sugar in a trash barrel on the way and pulls a set of keys from her back pocket. Not her keys. These have a small pocketknife and a Dallas Cowboys star dangling from them.

Mom has the driver's door of Mr. Guillory's car, a cream-colored vintage Mercury Comet, open in seconds. She reaches across the bench seat and pushes open the passenger door for me.

"You took his keys? Why would you do that?"

The streetlight overhead catches the sharp lines in her face. "Katelyn, get in the car. We don't have time for this."

I know Mom is the way she is because she loves me and wants something for me that she never had as a kid: safety. That's why I've never refused to follow her rules; I've just bent them. And, yeah, I still have to deal with her paranoia, but I can tell she tries really hard to keep that from me as much as possible. So I've gone along with her social media ban and her need to vet every new friend I make.

All in all, I think I'm pretty easygoing, but stealing our neighbor's car? It's so just plain wrong that it overrides the numb confusion that was keeping me silent.

"We can't just take Mr. Guillory's car. Why can't we take our car? Or better yet, why do we have to leave at all?"

"We'll make sure he gets it back, but—"

An alarm blares behind me. From our house.

Mom's eyes bulge as she stares over my shoulder, and for the first time in my entire life, I hear my mother swear. Then she says, "We're too late."

DRIVE

We're too late.

I have no idea what that means.

All I know is that Mom looks like we're in the direct path of a tornado. I glance back toward our house and see someone moving past the bedroom windows upstairs.

I get in the car.

"Please," I say in a voice that has gone suddenly hoarse. "*What* is going on?"

Mom peels out of the driveway instead of answering, looking more at the mirrors than the windshield in front of her. I crane my neck around and see a shadowed figure leap out from Mr. Guillory's backyard. It starts running after us.

We sideswipe a parked car and then careen onto the sidewalk as Mom makes a sharp turn, wrestling with the older car's lack of power steering. "Put your seat belt on."

My hands are shaking so badly that it takes two tries before

I can fasten it. I don't see the other car before it slams into us, sending my head smacking into the window hard enough to cause spots behind my eyes. I blink at the shocking pain and the shower of glass that rains down on me. The other car separates from ours—Mr. Guillory's—and the scene comes back into focus with a crunch of metal.

"You all right? Katelyn, answer me!" The car spins as she brakes suddenly and shifts into drive.

"I'm okay." But of course I'm not. I've never been less okay in my life. Even once she loses the other car after several terrifying minutes, Mom continues to check all her mirrors in a pattern of rapid glances that make my head throb viciously trying to follow. I don't say anything else, even some twenty minutes later when she pulls into a Walgreens parking lot.

"I'll be back in eight minutes. Do not move."

And she leaves me there. I watch her walk past half a dozen cars before she stumbles, catches herself on the hood of a white minivan, and throws up. Then she straightens and walks into the store.

Dazed, and bleeding from dozens of tiny cuts along my arms, I feel something warm and wet trickling down the side of my head. I touch it, then look at my fingers and barely have enough time to fling my door open before I'm sick.

I give up trying to get the crumpled door shut afterward, instead staring into space, in total disbelief. I've only just resolved to try again when I see Mom emerging from the store, laden with bulging plastic bags. She walks not to her door but to mine, opening it fully without difficulty. She slides a hand around my back and helps me out, carefully avoiding my vomit. My head spins, but at least I'm not sick again.

She holds up a set of keys with the hand that's not supporting me, and the double beep of a car unarming sounds. Mom leads me to the passenger seat of this new vehicle—something silver—and buckles me in. She hesitates for a second before shutting my door, clearly looking at the blood that has dripped onto my shoulder. "You'll be fine," she says, jerking her chin firmly, but I can hear the bags shaking as she loads them into the backseat.

I feel so far from fine, especially when I see the massive supply of protein bars and water bottles, and enough first-aid supplies to open a hospital. Mom slides into the driver's seat.

"We're stealing another car," I say. I must be in shock. No way I could have spoken so calmly otherwise. "Some customer we don't even know."

"No." She adjusts the mirrors and pulls out of the parking lot. "Not a customer, an employee." Before I can ask what difference that makes, she goes on. "A customer would finish shopping a lot sooner than an employee would finish their shift. Hopefully. I need at least two hours before this vehicle is reported stolen."

My hands feel like ice. "I don't . . ." My teeth begin to chatter. Mom turns on the heater and aims the vents at me.

"Katelyn, I'm so sorry." She takes a deep breath. "I don't even know where to start. . . ."

The events run through my head as she speaks: Someone broke into our house. We stole a car.

"But I'm going to keep you safe."

Someone tried to run us off the road. We stole another car.

"I need you to do exactly what I say, and I promise everything will be okay."

"Mom, who were those people, and why were they"—the thought of the car slamming into us sends ice water trickling down my spine—"after us?" Talking makes my head pound, but I knew not asking the questions would hurt worse.

Everything I say makes her wince. "I will explain what I can, but I can't do that while I'm driving. Right now, I need to get us somewhere safe and I need to think." She glances at me. "Please, Katelyn."

I want to give her that, but I can't. "Should I be this scared?"

She's supposed to say no. "I won't let anyone hurt you." She pauses for what feels like an eternity. "And I'm the person who loves you more than anyone else alive."

My head hurts badly enough to make it difficult to think clearly. "Are we in some kind of witness relocation program?" She knew to run. She knows how to steal a car without getting caught. She's not shaking at all anymore. "Mom? Why do you know how to do all this?"

She breaks her pattern of checking the mirrors to look at

me. "No, we're not in witness protection. I made a mistake when I was younger, and I had to learn."

I make the mistake of turning in my seat to check the road behind us, and my head makes it feel like the car is spinning around me. It takes a full minute of focused breathing before I can speak again. "A mistake? What kind of mistake?"

"The kind I can't run from anymore."

HIDE

Several hours later, I'm not even sure what state we're in when Mom pulls into a roadside motel with a forest of birch trees behind it. The building is nondescript, save for the flashing neon sign of a girl diving into a pool, and it's remote enough to be unsettling without the circumstances that led us there. The closest sign of civilization is a tiny strip mall we passed a mile back, whose highlights included a pawnshop, a secondhand clothing store, and a gas station with only one working pump. Mom smooths her hair and checks her lipstick in the rearview mirror before climbing out and telling me to stay in the car.

"Your shirt," I say, and she pauses with the door open to look down at the blood on her shoulder. My blood from when we'd switched cars at Walgreens.

She removes the pins holding up her long auburn hair and arranges it carefully over one shoulder. Then she's gone, disappearing into the office and returning minutes later with a key for room 5.

The chill from the air conditioner sets my teeth chattering again, and I let Mom steer me to the bed and sit me down on the salmon-colored bedspread. The curtains are already drawn, but she pulls them together again before hanging the Do Not Disturb sign on the outside knob.

She leaves me again but returns quickly, carrying my backpack, her duffel, and the bags from her eight-minute shopping trip. She speaks while she removes various first-aid items and starts cleaning the nicks on my arms before moving to my head. Warm fingers prod around the source of the pain along my temple. "I can't take you to a hospital. We're going to have to do the best we can on our own. It's not deep, but I have no way to stitch you up, so it's likely going to scar." Her fingers slide an inch to my hairline. "Are you dizzy?"

"Not as much as I was."

"Good."

It takes another five minutes before she sits back at my feet and lifts her hand to chew on her thumbnail, a gesture so familiar in such an unfamiliar situation that I get a lump in my throat. "You may have a concussion."

I'd had one once before, from falling out of a tree. This feels worse. "You promised to explain. Mom—"

"Stop." Her back snaps tight. "There isn't time to tell you everything. I need to get rid of that car and—"

"Then tell me some of it. Anything." She doesn't want to, that much is obvious, but perhaps because I'm literally bleeding in front of her, she starts talking.

"I've been hiding for a very long time, since before I had you."

"Did Dad know?"

She hesitates, as though the answer might reveal more than she wants. "He . . . No, he didn't know." The bed dips as she sits next to me. "I was careful, always careful. Sometimes I could almost believe they weren't looking anymore—" She bites off whatever she was going to say next. "But now it's different. We can't hide. They know what we look like, where we live. . . ."

Because I showed them. That's what she isn't saying. I created a dating profile with a picture of the two of us standing in front of the house they'd broken into. There was no house number in the photo; it was mostly a tree and the side of the house. And I didn't even use her full name. But someone found us. Less than two hours after I posted it.

That isn't possible. People can't be found like that, can they?

I'm going to be sick again.

She brushes the hair back from my head again, careful not to press too hard. "With a concussion, you need to be woken up every hour, so I'm going to set an alarm on this phone." She moves to reach into another bag and presses a disposable cell phone into my hand. I try to give it back to her.

"Why can't you just wake me?" I clamp my free hand

24

down on her forearm when she doesn't answer right away. "Mom?"

She flinches. "Because I have to go." She extricates herself from my grip. "Listen carefully: You are not to leave this room for any reason. Do not open the door. Do not peer out the window. Do not use the room phone. Do not answer the room phone. Do not make outgoing calls on this phone." She hesitates, then rips the cord out of the wall. If I were inclined to ignore her demands—which I'm not—she just took the choice from me. "It's only for a few days. I'll call you as soon as I can."

I stare at her. "You're not seriously leaving me? Why can't we go to the police?"

"Because the police can't help us!"

I recoil at the sudden volume of her voice.

In a softer tone, she says, "I'm sorry, but there's no time anymore. There are people looking for us right now. Think how fast they found us from that profile. They probably already have Mr. Guillory's car, which means they are way too close to finding that car." She points behind her to the silver car parked outside our room. "I have to go, and you aren't coming with me. You can't."

My jaw is quivering. "*You* can't just leave me like this. You haven't told me anything. Why are we hiding? Who is chasing us? How do you know about stealing cars?"

She keeps silent, checking the room again, drawing the curtains still further closed, looking everywhere but at me.

"Please take me with you," I say. But my pleading had no effect; it never does. Not when I'm begging to stay out an hour later or to get a ride with a friend whose car she hasn't inspected. Her paranoia is making a scary kind of sense now, but it's also contagious.

"No, you'll be safe here if you do what I say. Do you understand?"

All I understand is that my mom has been lying to me my entire life. "If you leave, how am I supposed to be safe? I don't know *anything*!"

She stops when I practically scream that last word, turning to look at me for the first time in minutes. Her gaze lingers on the bandage on my head before lowering to the drops of blood on my shirt. Her fingers twitch at her side, and she's taking a step toward me before she can stop herself. And then she's holding me, stroking my head.

"If there was any other way, I would take it. I made a mistake. When the time is right, I—not you—will be the one to pay for it." She pulls back enough to meet my gaze without fully letting me go. "And if I didn't think you were strong enough or smart enough for me to leave you . . ." She looks up and blinks her eyes dry before meeting mine again. "You have to be strong right now. We both do. I know you're scared and confused, but every second counts. Tell me you understand that, Katelyn." She shakes me a little when she says my name.

The past few hours, I've been so busy drowning in my

own fear that I didn't consider hers, not really. She never seemed scared the way I was. She made each decision without seeming to agonize over it, and she acted quickly, efficiently. But this close to her now, when I can feel each tremble in her body and how cold her hands are on my shoulders, I know her fear is every bit as consuming as mine. It might be even more so, because she's not just thinking of herself; she's thinking of me.

Always.

Every move. Every rule. Every over-the-top paranoid act. She's been protecting me, preparing me.

For this.

My head is throbbing too much to nod, but I say the truth she needs to hear. "I understand."

She squeezes my shoulders, and her chin quivers once before she forces down her emotion and stands. "The room is paid for, and you have enough food and water for at least a week, but this will all be over before then." She keeps talking, repeating the rules she already told me, and I realize she doesn't want to leave me any more than I want her to go.

"Okay," I say, cutting her off. "I'll stay here, no interaction of any kind with anyone. I won't—I won't mess up this time." I stare hard at the disposable phone, not trusting myself to look at her. "As soon as you're gone, I'll call Regina to cover for me at work, and I'm supposed to meet Carmel tomorrow to study for our history test on Monday, but—"

"No, you can't call anyone." Her fingers dig into my shoulders. "Not anyone. They found us from a photo. A *photo*. Don't think for a minute that they aren't watching everyone we know."

"But I'll lose my job, and I promised Carmel we'd cover the St. Bartholomew's Day Massacre. She keeps forgetting who the Huguenots were, and . . . and . . ." I'm tripping over my words, trying to get them out fast enough for her to understand. I can't just disappear. We've finally stayed put long enough that people will care if I'm suddenly gone one day. And what about Aiden? He'll be waiting for me outside the library, where we always meet. If I don't show up, he'll think I'm giving him his answer, that I don't care about him the way he cares about me.

I'll crush him, and I don't want to do that. I don't want to do any of this.

I feel my chin tremble, and then Mom has her arms around me again.

"I'm sorry. I didn't want this for you, and I'm going to make it right. I promise I will."

My throat goes tight. I ask the question that no one should ever have to ask her mom: "What if something happens to you?"

She's silent for so long that I start hearing the pounding of my heartbeat.

She opens her mouth, closes it, then opens it again. "I don't have a choice anymore." She hugs me then, and the pressure makes me feel sick again, but I hug her back just as tightly.

"Just tell me—who's after you?" I ask when she moves to the door.

She stops with her hand on the knob, and even though I can't see her face, I know her eyes are squeezed shut when she answers. "Whatever happens, please remember I love you."

ESCAPE

Mom doesn't call.

The first day, I tell myself there are a lot of things that might have delayed her. Maybe she had car trouble. Maybe she lost her phone or the battery died. Maybe whatever she's doing is taking longer than she thought.

Maybe a million things that don't mean anything is wrong.

But also, maybe she's hurt.

Maybe they found her.

Maybe they killed her.

I don't sleep.

The second day, I don't do as good a job lying to myself. Mom should have called. Whatever else she's hidden from me, her love isn't one of them. She wouldn't leave me like this, alone for days, unless she had no choice.

Because she was hurt.

Because they found her.

Because they killed her.

I chew all ten of my fingernails to the quick. I don't stop even when they bleed.

I huddle on the corner of the bed and rock.

⌇

In the middle of the night, I take the cell phone apart. I haven't slept in two days, and the idea of action, any action, is too hard to ignore. There must be a defect or something that won't let her call get to me. It's a delusion, but I cling to it fiercely until I'm surrounded by electronic wreckage and my cheeks are stained with tears.

⌇

It's been three days since I've seen or spoken to another living soul.

Three days.

I spend most of the day reassembling the cell phone, because why did I think I could take it apart and put it back together again like that? When I'm left with a phone that looks more or less the way it started, I turn it on. The display lights up with a welcome chime, and I want to hurl it against the wall.

Instead, I break Mom's first rule: I leave the motel room. I don't go far, but every step makes me feel like I'm in the cross-hairs of a dozen enemies. Still, exhaustion mutes my panic, and I have no other choice. I have to know.

There's a decrepit-looking pay phone fifty feet away—less, even—but it takes an eternity to reach it. Then several more eternities as I feed it change and dial the number for my cell. And when it rings loud and clear across the parking lot, no connection problems whatsoever, my knees give out.

I'm kneeling on the asphalt with my arm hanging from the cord of the phone above me when I realize:

I'm alone.

＜

The walls seem to flee from me the second I step back inside, withdrawing the semblance of safety I'd felt from them when I still believed Mom would return.

Something happened, full stop. I refuse to let my brain hurl itself farther than that one fact. Mom had to change her plans, which means I have to change mine.

The cell phone is in my hand again, and I've half dialed Regina's number before the muscles in my forearm seize up, stopping me. We were both scheduled at the café that after-noon, and it's just after three, which means she'll have worked up the courage to squeak a single "hi" to Evan, the new busboy, before dashing off without giving him a chance to respond. I'd bet money on her being in the third bathroom stall from the right at that exact moment, systematically shredding a single square of toilet paper while wishing I was there to give her the report about which side of his mouth had smiled higher in response and whether he'd looked disappointed or relieved that she'd run off.

He was disappointed—always disappointed—and I was so close to getting her to stand still for more than a second so he could say hi back.

Instead, I wasn't there. I never showed up or even called. The disposable cell phone in my hand turned heavy. My phone, the one I'd been forced to leave, along with more of my life than I'd even realized, was no doubt flooded with texts and missed calls from her and Carmel.

Aiden.

I was supposed to meet him two days ago.

I keep expecting you to just ghost me one of these days.

The phone slips through my fingers and clatters to the floor. That's what he said to me, and now that's exactly what I've done. I can see his face, his ever-present easy, warm smile dimming as the minutes ticked past and I failed to show. He would have sent texts too, making sure I was okay.

By now, would he have decided his prediction had come true?

And I can't even contact him and explain. Or Regina. Or Carmel or anyone. That's why my muscles seized. I don't know what a call from me might do to them.

Better they think I flaked out.

Blew her off.

Broke his heart without a single care.

I wrap my arms around myself and suck in a shaky breath. "Mom, where are you?"

⁓

The walls never get any closer no matter what I do to mentally shorten the distance between them. Counting off the number of paces from side to side doesn't help, but something else does. Ever since I can remember, Mom and I had a ritual for whenever we moved to a new place. Before we unpacked our bags or picked our bedrooms, we played a game where I had to find the way out of every room. When I was little, it was as easy as pointing out windows or doors. But when I got older, it wasn't enough to identify the basement window I'd use. Mom made me show her how I'd reach it, pry it open when it was inevitably stuck, and show her how quickly and quietly I could get out. Just in case.

Mom always said it was the Girl Scout in her that kept her so vigilant.

Girl Scout, my ass.

There are only two rooms in this motel room. The bedroom has the front door and two large windows, but the bathroom has only a small window above the toilet, one of those pull-out deals with hinges at the bottom, which are held in place by rusted screws that make my fingers throb just to look at them.

It'll take hours to loosen them, assuming I even can. And I don't want to. I want to go back to the bed and curl into a ball and sleep until Mom wakes me up and tells me this has all been a bad dream.

The toilet seat creaks when I step up on it, and the rust digs into my fingertips as I start twisting. It ends up taking just over an hour, and I sacrifice two fingernails to the cause before the final screw gives up its fight. I leave the last one loose but in place and trail back to the bedroom.

I avoid the bed, since planning for exits didn't feel anything like a game this time and I'm too afraid to sleep. Instead, I slide to the floor and stare at Mom's engagement ring, a gaudy piece of costume jewelry that my dad found at a flea market. I've worn it on a delicate chain around my neck for years. I try to catch the light on the many facets until I fall asleep or, more accurately, pass out. I dream about Aiden climbing through my window and Mom catching him in my bedroom. I know it's a dream because she invites him to stay for dinner, and I keep jumping throughout the meal whenever somebody clinks a fork against their plate.

A car door slamming in the parking lot jolts me awake. Tucking the ring beneath my shirt, I break another one of Mom's rules by dashing to a front window and moving a curtain aside to peer out. I leave the sheer one in place, so everything I see outside is hazy as the last sliver of the sun slips below the horizon, but I can tell that the person in the driver's seat of the car outside is definitely not my mom. I don't have time to register the sharp agony of disappointment, because Mom's paranoia is seeping into my pores. It's like my eyes have finally been opened to the world for the very first time.

The last person I saw besides my mom was someone trying to run us off the road.

All I can think now is that danger is only a pane of glass away.

A lump forms in my throat, and I want to sink to the floor. I can't pretend that she's coming back for me anymore, that I don't have to protect myself because she'll do it for me. Something has gone very wrong with her plan. The lump swells, but I force it down. If she were with me in this room, I know what she'd tell me to do. So I start breathing and thinking, moving almost before deciding I'm going to.

I scoop up a chair, dragging it across the carpet to block the door. As a barrier, it'll provide nothing more than a few seconds' delay, but if someone comes through the motel room door, I'm going to need every advantage I can get. I want to add more chairs, to build a mountain of them between whoever is outside and me, but no amount of furniture will save me if I'm still here when they come in. It already feels like ages since the car door slammed.

I have no reason to feel safer once I'm in the bathroom, but I do. Just being in here buys me a few more seconds. They'll have to search for me.

I stand on the toilet, and the screw I left in earlier takes barely a turn to pop free into my hand. I lower the window to the counter and peer outside to ensure there's no one there. I pull myself up and begin the Houdini-like task of squeezing myself through. I'm not as slight as my mom, and so I get stuck almost immediately.

My hands are frantic, searching for something to grab and use as leverage, and I imagine someone bursting into the room and finding me like this. But fear is a great motivator. I shimmy around and exhale every scrap of air that ever entered my lungs. My jeans catch on the window frame and I hear a rip, and I hiss when my hip scrapes along a jagged edge. But I don't stop. If anything, I redouble my efforts.

Someone is at the door. I hear the knob turning, gently at first, then with more force.

I brace my hands on the exterior wall and push as hard as I can. Harder. I pop free and slam down, a good seven feet below, onto the chewed-up asphalt. Blood trickles from my elbows and my hip, but the pain barely registers. The door to room 5 is rattling, and then *bang*. A crack reverberates through the entire building as the door is kicked in. I'm choking on my own heart as I shoot to my feet and run.

FLEE

The pavement behind the motel slopes into a ditch, which I skid down before tumbling into the densely packed forest of birch trees. The jagged bark catches my clothes and hair as I run, pulling at me, slowing me down. And I can't make myself stay quiet. My breath comes in strangled gasps. *Help me.*

The ground is wet and muddy from the rain the night before, causing me to slip over and over. Each time I get to my feet, I'm sure I'll see the person after me, but I can barely see at all. The sun is setting fast, and I can't make out anything more than ten feet in any direction in the murky darkness of the forest.

I scramble over a fallen tree and lie flat, pressing my side against the bark. I force myself into silence, but my body doesn't want to obey. My lungs burn and my pulse pounds, and nowhere near enough air billows in and out through my nose.

Then I hear it. On my exposed side, someone moving through the trees.

Faster than me.

Terror closes its icy hand around my heart, squeezing tighter and tighter as the footsteps draw nearer.

It takes everything I have not to bolt and tear through that mass of trees like the devil himself was after me. I want to flee like nothing I've ever wanted before. The impulse is so strong I have to constantly command my tensing muscles to slow down. I creep on my belly around the fallen birch, scanning ahead for small twigs that might snap under my weight. When I'm on the other side, I make myself wait. I squeeze my eyes shut as the footsteps grow louder, then grow quieter again, moving past me and deeper into the forest.

My eyes dart everywhere. To my right is shadow, but to my left, I think I see the trees beginning to thin.

Maybe there's open field, where my pursuer can pick me off from their post in the trees.

Maybe it's a ravine, and I'll plummet to my death before I see the edge.

Maybe I'm delirious, and the tress aren't thinning at all.

If I run that way, I'll be exposed in seconds, and I refuse to bet my life on what might or might not be on the other side of those trees. But I can't stay cowering on the forest floor either.

My breathing is growing choppy again as an idea forms. It's not a good idea, but being overtaken in the woods—or the unknown beyond them—by someone faster is worse. And the reality is that I'm gambling with my life no matter what I do. So I choose the high reward.

And turn back toward the motel.

I give full reign to my flight instinct, scurrying from tree to tree, pausing at every trunk to listen for my pursuer, hopefully still moving in the opposite direction. But I hear only the blood pumping in my ears, and I move like I can feel the breath of every nightmare I've ever had panting down my neck.

And to what? I might be heading toward another threat, one that's waiting patiently for me to return. That's the kind of paralyzing fear I have to strangle in its crib.

I am going back to the motel because I know nothing about who's after me. I know nothing about where Mom is or what she's doing. I know nothing about why I'm running for my life. But I do know that there is a car parked in front of my room and that the driver knew where to find me. There could be someone else lying in wait, an accomplice ready to grab me or worse, but there could also be something inside the car, something that might lead me to Mom and the answers I need. At the very least, I might be able to slip back into the room and grab my bag. Right now, I have to believe the reward outweighs the risk.

A fresh wave of dread crashes over me when I reach the tree line and the back of the motel comes into view, but I don't have time to second-guess my decision. I pry my fingers from the tree I'm clinging to, and I step out into the open.

Thankfully, there are lots of shadows to shield me as I walk. I home in on the car in front of room 5, a dark-blue Honda Accord with band stickers on the bumper and a parking pass for Penn State stuck to the windshield. The car's innocuous appearance is somehow more terrifying than the black armored car I was prepared for.

My heart is close to detonating by the time I reach the driver's side, approaching from behind. The headrest is tall and solid, so I can't tell, I can't tell. . . .

The car is empty. I lean forward against the side, boneless with relief. Then I look up at the kicked-in door to my motel room. The wood is splintered around the lock, and the chain is glinting on the carpet inside. And my fear slinks back up, coiling around my ankles, knees, stomach, all the way to my throat.

What am I thinking? I'm about to break into the car of the person who broke down my door, who chased me through the woods, and who very possibly tried to run us off the road three nights ago. . . .

I don't have a lockpicking tool, and I wouldn't know how to use one if I did. What I do have is a big-ass rock and zero concern for property damage. I'm trying to decide how far back to stand when another thought occurs to me. I reach out to try the door handle.

It opens.

I leap in and pull the door only partially closed. I have to be ready for a quick escape if I need to run again, and I'm not wasting any time opening the door. My other idea involves slipping out and rolling under the car to hide if the driver comes out of the woods. There are so many problems with that, though—like what's to stop him from running me over when he backs up and sees me? My skull will burst like a watermelon. I force the image away and start searching the car.

I flip down both visors, and a flood of concert tickets flutters into my lap. The console is filled with change and a few petrified french fries. I lean forward to open the glove compartment and find tons of takeout napkins, a pair of gloves, and a registration certificate that says the vehicle belongs to a Malcolm Pike.

There's nothing about Mom. No incriminating papers. I slam the glove compartment shut.

A thud from behind me strangles my sob. I jump and whip around, but there's nothing.

Then another thud, and my stomach lurches.

There's someone in the trunk.

EVADE

I fly out the door, almost tripping over my own feet. Mom. It has to be Mom. I dive back to the driver's seat before I'm halfway to the trunk. There has to be a latch somewhere. Half sitting in the car, I find it on the console and I crane my neck to see the trunk release. I dart back and lift it open.

With my arms stretching high above my head to open the trunk, and the fragile fluttery hope that I'm about to find Mom, I'm not prepared for the two-footed kick that hits me square in the chest. The impact throws me off my feet with enough force to knock the wind out of me. I hurl backward to the ground, and there's a *thwack* as my head makes contact with the asphalt. I watch through watering eyes as the occupant of the trunk heaves bound legs over the edge, then crashes down next to me.

I can't seem to breathe or move, and my brain feels like

it must be scattered halfway across the parking lot. Gasping as air finally gushes back into my deflated lungs, I roll to my stomach and push up onto my hands and knees. I grab the phone that flew out of my pocket, cursing the shattered screen, and hurriedly repocket it. My pulse is racing and my head is throbbing as I take in the trunk's occupant clearly for the first time.

It's a lean black guy in a hoodie and skinny jeans. And he's gagged, with his hands tied behind his back. His eyebrow is split open, though whether that's from when he was tossed in the trunk or when he fell out of it, I can't tell. He's squinting into the setting sun as he ineffectively thrashes around trying to free himself. He can't see me from his angle on the ground, and I realize he probably didn't see me before trying to kick my sternum out through my back. I doubt he saw more than a silhouette.

He probably thought I was the person who put him there in the first place.

"It's okay," I wheeze through lungs that are still readjusting. "I'm not . . . He's in the woods, but he could come back at any moment, so we have to hurry." I scramble forward, placing a hand on his back to let him know I'm there, since he hasn't managed to roll over and see me yet. His hands are bound tight with one of those thick plastic zip ties, and I have no idea how I'm supposed to get it off. I'm reluctant to prod it too much, since the surrounding skin is raw and bleeding, evidence of how desperately he's been trying to free himself. Larger zip ties lock his ankles together.

The skin between my shoulder blades is starting to itch; anyone could be coming up behind me. I should be running away, apologizing that I can't help. Mom is still out there somewhere, and she's in at least as much danger as I am, if not more.

But I don't run; instead I start examining the ground, searching for any reasonably sharp rocks that might work to cut him free.

The itch between my shoulders has become a jagged, clawing scrape.

"Do you have anything I can use? A pocketknife maybe?" I don't wait for an answer—not that he could have given me one anyway, with the gag knotted around his mouth—before shoving my hands in his back pockets. I find his wallet and a folded-up photo, which falls onto the ground beside me. More nothing.

I can't leave him here. But I also can't stay.

My gaze is ricocheting everywhere, searching for a solution as I repocket his wallet, when it stops on the photo. I unfold it, and my whole body goes still.

It's the picture of me and Mom that I posted to the dating site. But it's not a printout; it's the actual photo. The one that hung framed in the stairway at home. I know because the frame I bought was too small and I used the only pair of scissors I could find at the time—Mom's scalloped craft scissors—to cut it to size. I run my finger along the wavy edge, and it's like another kick to the chest.

Still on my hands and knees, I move sideways until I'm in the bound guy's line of sight. One of his eyes is in the process of swelling shut, but the other goes wide when he sees my face. He recognizes me, which sends me scurrying backward.

He's trying to say something, but his gag is tight. And it doesn't matter, because all I hear in my head is *He knows me.*

He was in my house.

He's trying to inch toward me but making little progress, and he's repeating the same muffled sounds over and over.

My teeth clench of their own accord. I have never felt such an overwhelming urge to hurt someone. I never understood the "blood boiling" metaphor before, but it is perfection. I am burning inside and out, and I could claw his twitching eye out.

"Where is my mom, and why are you after us?" My lips hardly move as I spit my questions at him. "How do you know me?" My fists grow tighter and tighter at my sides. But of course, he can't answer me, gagged like that. He can barely move with those ties cinched around his ankles and wrists.

I shoot a glance to the trees. I have no idea how much time has passed; it could have been seconds or minutes. What I do know is that this guy is the only lead I've found, and he can't hurt me as long as he's tied up.

"Come on," I say, scrambling toward him and slipping an arm around his back. I get him sitting, then to his knees. He keeps up his muffled yells the entire time. "I'm not wasting time on your gag right now." It's not just tape that I can rip off; it's tightly knotted cloth that'll have to be cut. "Now move!" I use the same inflection Mom did to get me out of the house. It works. He rocks back on his heels and stands. He's taller than me and heavier, but he's coming with me, even if I have to drag him.

And there's no time to think anything through. We need to get out of sight, hide somewhere until whoever is searching for me gives up and leaves. Then I can get my answers.

Close. I need somewhere close. I look around, my gaze landing on the wrecked motel room almost immediately, taking in the long salmon-colored bedspread that drapes nearly to the ground. I tell myself that whoever broke the door down isn't going to search the room again after chasing me through the woods. It's vaguely comforting, and the only thought I have time for. I hiss another command at the guy I'm supporting and close the trunk and car door before guiding his hopping and wincing body inside.

Once we're there, I force him to his knees and topple him onto his shoulder. I'm pretty sure he's swearing at me, but I don't care. Soon it won't matter.

He's too heavy for me to lift on my own, but he finally seems to understand what I want from him, and he rolls onto his stomach before shimmying under the bed. A few days ago, I'd have been overcome with concern for his shoulders, with his hands tied behind his back like that. Now, I brace a foot on the wall behind me and shove.

He's under the bed as much as our combined efforts can get him, so I dart around to the other side and slide next to him. Only a sliver of light reaches us with the bedspread pulled straight.

So then we wait. And I pray.

WATCH

I'm sweaty from the terror-filled sprint through the woods, scratched from the many branches I didn't dodge, and bleeding, from both the trees and my window dive. My eyes feel like they're trying to leap out of my skull, and I have no confidence that I'll be able to calm down. Ever. My chest aches and my head is throbbing, and now I'm inches away from the person responsible for that pain—and potentially so much more.

With the small bit of light creeping under the bedspread, I can see a rough outline of his face. He's still trying to communicate around his gag in something like a whisper.

I want him to shut up. We need to be quiet, silent. We are children hiding beneath a bed, and the monster is coming. Every sound from outside is an approach, in my mind, and the incessant murmurings next to me are going to lead my pursuer straight to us. I can't risk even a whispered command to tell him to be quiet. But I do slide my hand across my stomach, up his shoulder, and over his mouth. Then I push down, bringing my face as close as possible in the small space afforded us. I shake my head and push harder. I can tell my eyes are wild in their sockets, and I let him see them.

When he finally falls silent, I wait another thirty seconds, to make sure he understands that he needs to stay that way, and then I return my hand to my side.

The new silence kicks at me, twitching my muscles and roiling my stomach. I have nothing, no weapon to defend myself, nothing to lash out with. I don't even have an escape route if I need one. I'm on the far side of the bed, opposite the door. If I'm found, I have nowhere to run. I won't have time to squeeze through the bathroom window again. I don't even have the confidence that I'd be able to fit a second time.

The sting along my hip reasserts itself, and I let my fingers graze over the raw skin. The entire right hip of my jeans is hanging across my thigh. Next to me, the guy jerks, and then the dim light under the bed parts. And a new shadow moves.

I didn't hear the approaching footsteps. I didn't feel anything except my own misery. Did my pursuer hear me? Panic coils through my ribs and cinches tight until I taste vomit, sour and strong in the back of my throat. How can terror spike again and again and reach new peaks every time?

The booted feet draw nearer to the bed. The same ones that kicked down the door and chased me through the woods less than an hour ago. The guy hiding with me can't see what

I can. His head is turned toward me, and his eyes are darting around like a feral animal. I move my hand across the space separating us and press it against his. His eyes stop darting immediately and meet mine.

I don't know why I did it. To keep him quiet? To stop him from doing something that would get us caught? To stop myself? I do know that it seems to calm both of us.

The boots move past the bed. The man wearing them digs through my backpack, then trails over to the bags Mom left me. He upends them one at time, spilling the protein bars and water bottles all over the floor. He kicks at them, and then he kneels to rummage through the leftover first-aid supplies, sifting through all the unused gauze and tape. He picks up the bottle of painkillers and checks the contents before tossing it back to the floor and standing. The bottle rolls under the bed and comes to a stop at my calf, causing my stomach to leap into the roof of my mouth.

The hand against mine presses silently back. I tear my gaze away from the boots to meet the eyes of the guy next to me. It's nearly dark outside, so the only illumination is a glow from the lights in the parking lot, but it's enough to see him, and to feel the reassurance from the presence of another person.

I pull my hand back to my hip and blink, needing to keep my vision sharp as I track the boots moving farther away. They walk into the bathroom, then back out a few seconds later. He's not searching, not really. He doesn't suspect I'm here. And why would he? I'm still in the woods or beyond them, faster than he thought, but not back here. Nothing is here except failure.

My pulse skips in my veins, not as hot as rage or as cold as terror. He didn't find me, and he's not going to. He's leaving.

When the car door slams outside, we both jump. Seconds later, the engine roars to life.

He's gone.

I'm safe.

He's gone.

I'm safe.

The guy next to me is shimmying again, trying to get out from under the bed, but with incredible difficulty. I slide out from my side and cross over to his. The desperate urgency to get him hidden is gone, so I take more care in helping him out. When he's sitting upright against the side of the bed frame, I go to prop up what's left of the motel door. It doesn't look good, but at least it will draw less attention than an entirely missing door.

I look back over my shoulder at my . . . what? Captive? Escapee? Guy who may or may not be in as much danger as I am? Adrenaline has been coursing through me since that first car door slam, but now I'm just weary, which, on top of frayed nerves, means I'm nowhere near as ruthless and decisive as I was in the parking lot.

And I need to be.

Because I'm about to cut the gag from his mouth. And he knows something. Maybe about Mom, definitely about the man who left empty-handed. I just have to ask the right questions.

INTERROGATE

I move toward him cautiously; his eyes follow my every step. When I kneel in front of him and get a good look at his gag, I see just how desperate he's been to get it off. The corners of his mouth are still bleeding, unlike the scabs on the rest of his face. I hesitate as I lift my hands.

How long has it been? The sun is down, so thirty minutes? An hour? He's had time to think about what he's going to say to me. Enough time to tell me exactly what he wants.

I swallow. I don't know how to interrogate someone. I'll have no way of knowing if he's lying, and he's definitely going to be inclined to lie if it'll get me to cut him loose.

I reach behind his head, ignoring the tacky dampness that brushes my skin, and start working on the knots. "We both know that the guy in the boots is going to come back when he doesn't find me, and then he might not be alone. If I think you're lying to me at any point, I have no problem leaving you here for him." Can he feel my hands trembling? "I'm not going to cut you free. So don't ask me to. Answer my questions, and I promise to call the motel after I'm gone and tell them where to find you." I wait for him to nod, even though it's a pointless response to a pointless statement. Innocent or not, he'll answer the same. And I have to remove the gag.

I gag when I get the fabric free. It's some kind of burlap, and it's crusted to the corners of his mouth. Fresh blood wells up when I peel it loose. But that's not the worst part. There's more fabric in his mouth, and a whole wad shoved partially down his throat. It's like a sadistic magic trick, pulling it all out.

He heaves, chokes, and heaves again before taking a full deep breath and speaking. Or trying to speak. He coughs and swallows, and I grab one of the water bottles that now litter the carpet. When I tip the bottle to his mouth, pinkish water runs down his chin and neck, soaking into the collar of his gray T-shirt and navy hoodie. He pulls away after a few swallows, to cough and retch some more, spitting blood onto the floor and . . . I don't know, part of a tooth? I try not to join him. I've never been so close to brutality like this, and it turns my stomach.

But a bigger part of me bats the empathy aside. Mom is gone, and people are chasing me. Quite possibly this guy's people.

He inclines his head for more water, and I give it to him. He drains half the bottle before he stops to breathe.

"Thank you," he says, his voice raspy and pained, "Katelyn."

The water bottle jerks in my hand at the sound of my name. Did I want him to lie about knowing me, about being complicit in this nightmare? Maybe I did.

"Who are you?"

"Can I have another sip of water?"

"No."

He strains against his bound wrists. They don't move, and he's smart enough not to ask me to free him. "My name is Malcolm Pike. I'm a sophomore at Penn State, computer science major. Or I was."

It was his car, his trunk he was in. "How do you know me, Malcolm Pike?"

He meets my eyes dead-on. "Because I was paid to find you. Actually, your mom."

I stand so I can look down at him, so I can feel like I'm in control and not like I want to hide under the bed again. "Paid by who?"

"Emily Abbott."

"I don't know who that is."

"Your mom does."

"Where is my mom?"

"If I knew that, I wouldn't be here."

I start to hyperventilate on the inside; outside, I lower to a squat in front of him. Up close, his face looks even worse. "I don't believe you."

"Join the club. Why do you think my face looks like this?"

It looks like he gave the wrong answers. Repeatedly. "Who are you?"

"I told you. Mal—"

"No. Who *are* you? Why were you in that trunk? Why were you searching for me? And who did you tell when you found me?" I lean closer. "Who are you, and who was that guy?"

He drops his head back against the bed. "It's a long story."

I stand up and retrieve the two snapped ends of the door chain, then drop them in his lap. "Tell it quickly."

Not just because we're on borrowed time, but also because my bravado is nearly exhausted. I won't be able to keep up this act much longer.

He eyes the broken chain like it could just as easily have been his body, and looking at his face, I'm inclined to agree. He's every bit as scared as I am. But none of that matters until he tells me what I need to know.

"That guy is a bounty hunter who thought he'd let me do the hard work of finding your mom, then swoop in and get me to lead him to her and claim the reward."

Cold sweat slicks over my skin. "Keep talking."

"Can we maybe get out of here first? I'll tell you every—" We both turn our heads to the motel door. A light flickers through one of the missing chunks near the lock. It flickers again, and I realize it's from a person moving back and forth just outside.

And then we hear them.

"Get away from there," a woman says.

"I think somebody kicked it down," a man replies, much closer, and the light stabbing into the room shifts again. "Look. See the boot scuff?"

"Yes, I do, which is why you need to get away from it."

"You think somebody is still in there?"

"I think I don't care," she says, her voice growing louder as she draws nearer. "Now are we getting a room or not?"

"Somebody could be hurt or dead inside. . . ."

"I'll tell you what," she says. "You can either spend your night screwing around with whoever's in that room, or . . ."

There is no missing her implication.

"Fine, but I'm telling the manager. Maybe he'll give us a discount."

"What do you mean *us*?" The clack of heels speeds up as she presumably hurries after him.

I turn back to Malcolm, and it's like he's read my mind. "You'll have to explain a lot more than a broken door if they find me like this." He shifts his shoulders to reveal his bound wrists.

He's right.

And I can't explain any of it.

The police would be called, which was, ironically, what I wanted from the beginning, except Mom said we couldn't go to the police. I stand and move to one of the front windows to peer through the gap in the curtains and watch the couple heading toward the office.

Malcolm has maneuvered himself to the other window by

the time I turn back. I'm both impressed and alarmed that he was able to get that far while being tied up. And I'm that much more certain I don't want to cut him free. But if we're going to get out of here, I don't have another choice.

I walk to the bathroom, dig my fingers under the razor-sharp window frame—the one that matches the slice on my hip—and pry one side loose.

Malcolm presses back into the wall when he sees me coming at him with the sharp piece of metal.

I kneel down at his side and reach around him. The angle is awkward; his shoulder digs into my chest as I saw through the zip tie around his wrists. "As soon as we're away from here, you are going to tell me everything." I can't back up my words with a threat, because once he's untied, I won't have much leverage at all. I move to the bindings on his ankles while he rubs the circulation back into his hands, carefully avoiding the bleeding red rings encircling each wrist.

"Days," he says, catching my stare. "I don't even know how long, but I doubt I would have made it to four if you hadn't helped me."

"And I wouldn't be running for my life if you hadn't pointed the way." I cut through the last tie on his ankles and glare at him. "Save your gratitude."

I leave him to get to his feet by himself and round up whatever looks potentially useful from the supplies strewn across the floor. I repack my backpack with the rest of the protein bars and as many of the first-aid supplies as I can carry. I'm not taking any grocery bags; I need both my hands free.

I grab my makeshift knife, crafted from the edge of the bathroom window, and make sure Malcolm sees me tuck it into the waistband of my jeans.

He limps toward the door, and I can't help wondering if he's playing up his injury so that I'll lower my guard. But he could be dragging himself across the floor with one arm, and I'd still bring the weapon with me.

I make a show of keeping my hand on it and nod my chin for Malcolm to precede me outside.

HOSTAGE

Malcolm's progress is slow once we're outside—too slow. I move to his left side, keeping the edge of the window-frame knife tucked on the outside and farthest from his grip, and sling his arm around my shoulder.

I decide he's not playing up how hurt he is. There is a fine sheen of sweat along his brow, and his lips draw tighter together with each step.

I tug his hoodie up over his head, hoping it'll provide enough shadow for his face in case anyone approaches. And I lean in close, trying to look like any other couple—albeit a drunk and staggering one—wrapped around each other and heading for our room. The performance is a pathetic one, but it doesn't raise an eyebrow from anyone we pass.

I spare a glance behind my shoulder once we're a few rooms away, and see three people exit from the main office: two men and a woman in very high heels. I don't need to see them point to the room we'd left behind to know who they are.

I'm grateful beyond words that Mom checked in without me. The manager won't look twice at Malcolm and me, or if he does, he won't connect us to the room with the busted-down door some twenty feet behind us. Still, I try to increase our speed, despite the very clear protests from the back of Malcolm's throat.

We finally round the corner of the motel and take a few more steps to the back. I help lower Malcolm to a sitting position against the wall, rather than drag him along with me any farther.

"I'm going to make sure they don't come looking this way. But don't try to run," I tell him. "I'm fast, and I will catch you. And then I'll be mad that you made me chase you."

I don't even recognize the words I'm saying, and my low, flat voice is starting to freak me out. I'm not particularly fast and I'm certainly not violent, and yet I must be doing a decent job of faking both those things, because Malcolm doesn't argue.

"Where am I gonna go?" He lifts one arm to gesture at the tree line nearby. No sign of civilization.

He doesn't look like he plans to willingly move anytime soon, but I know I'd run when given the chance, so I glance back at him every few seconds as I peer around the front of the motel. After several minutes, the three people emerge from our room and retrace their steps to the office.

When the couple reappears again, the man is swinging a room key around his index finger. The manager isn't far behind them, carrying a toolbox in one hand and a hammer in the other. He looks distinctly unhappy but also resigned.

I let my head drop against the side of the building in relief that he doesn't appear to have called the police. I pull the broken cell from my pocket; even I can tell it's beyond repair. My breath catches as I'm reminded again that this is the longest I've ever gone without talking to Mom. Why hasn't she come back? Why did she leave me alone with nothing but a crappy cell phone?

Something horrible must have happened to keep her from calling me. And even if she tries now, she won't reach me. The broken cell phone mocks me with its shattered screen, and it's only Malcolm's presence that keeps panic from closing in.

I don't want to go back to him, to tether any part of my future to his.

But now he's my only link to Mom.

Turning, I face Malcolm with an expression as dead as I feel. He hasn't moved. He isn't even watching me.

His eyes flutter open at the crunching gravel under my feet as I approach. "Are they still looking?"

"You don't get to ask me questions," I say. "The only reason you aren't still gagged in that motel room is because you have information I need."

He scowls at me, but I keep my face blank.

"Fine," he says. "You gonna interrogate me here, next to a dumpster?"

I don't want to. I want to get as far away from the motel as quickly as possible. But I want answers more. Fighting the trembling in my voice, I say, "Why are you searching for my mother?"

He licks his lips. "Look, maybe we should get out of here first."

He's stalling, or trying to, but not knowing is definitely worse than whatever he's not saying. I know my mom. Her "mistake" can't be as awful as the dread that's slowly devouring me. When I don't move, he sighs.

"Does the name Derek Abbott mean anything to you?"

I shake my head.

"His mother, Emily Abbott, is the one searching for your mom. The police could devote time and resources for only so long. After her husband passed away, Mrs. Abbott committed her fortune to funding a private manhunt—and she offered a reward to whoever locates and apprehends your mom."

A breeze kicks up, icy and stinging. It slaps against my face and pierces needles through my clothes. Denial catches in my throat when he says the words I'll never forget.

"She's wanted in the death of Derek Abbott."

REVEAL

"No." The word breaks off from my mouth. "That's not possible." I take a step backward, then another; Malcolm doesn't move. I want him to make a grab for me, to do something that exposes the lie I know he's just told me, but he doesn't.

"All parents have secrets," Malcolm says with a shrug. "Mine did."

"But my mom doesn't!" *Not big ones,* I amend to myself. "She would never—"

"Lie to you your entire life, abandon you in a motel, tell you next to nothing about what's happening? Why do you think she changed her name?"

"What?" I suck in a scrambled breath.

"So you didn't know that either. Awesome." He shakes his head back and forth before looking at me again and sighing. "Melissa Reed doesn't exist. Her real name is Tiffany Jablonski."

Something scuttles across my brain. Tiffany. I had a doll named Tiffany. Mom gave her to me when I was little. I remember she had dark-brown yarn hair. "Tiffany." When I say it out loud, it doesn't feel like my mom's name, not like Melissa does. "That can't be right." My brain is screaming at me. None of this makes sense, least of all that she killed someone. I think about the mistake Mom mentioned. Killing someone isn't a mistake.

"Are you sure?" Malcolm says, "'Cause I've seen the police report. Derek's autopsy—"

"Stop!" I say, my voice veering dangerously close to a shout. "You don't know anything. Not about me, and not about my mom. I don't know who Derek Abbott was or what my mom has to do with him, but she didn't kill anyone." There's a kind of calm that comes over me from just saying these words out loud. "What I do know is that you were with the man who came after me and that you had a picture in your pocket that used to hang in our stairway."

He lowers his gaze, and I can't tell if it's shame or merely a facade. Whichever it is, he stares straight at me again when he starts talking. "I took it when I was in your house on Friday night."

My gut twists at his admission. The last time I was in our house, I was teasing my mom about an awful first date and worrying that she'd figure out I'd snuck Aiden into my room.

Aiden doesn't even know what happened to me. Or what could still happen to me.

My gaze darts over Malcolm, his hoodie and jeans. I'd cut him loose without checking all his pockets. "Do you have a phone?"

"Sure," he says. "That guy wanted to make sure I could call for help in case it got too stuffy in the trunk."

I ignore his sarcasm and draw his attention back to the weapon I'm holding. "Get back against the wall."

"Go ahead and search me." He stands and tries to spread his arms but only gets the left one halfway up, hissing a breath through his teeth. "Don't get too cozy with my left side, though, yeah?"

There's nothing to do but get it over with. A phone could be the least potentially dangerous item in his possession. I place my makeshift knife on the ledge of the dumpster in case I need to grab for it; then I step up next him. "If you try—"

"You'll hurt me real bad. I remember your last threat. Hurry up and cop a feel so I can sit down." He shifts more of his weight against the wall and watches me.

I tilt my head. "Is this fun for you? Some kind of game? We had to flee my house that night, and we barely got away before people broke in—including you. Now, my mom is gone and whoever did that to your face is hunting me." I step closer. "Make your jokes. Go ahead."

He's silent after that.

I don't look at his face as I slip my hands into his pockets, front and back, then pat down his legs and around his ankles. I check the rest of his clothing too, but I find nothing except the wallet I came across earlier.

He tugs his hoodie back into place when I'm done. "You're right, it's not a game. I'm happy to be out of my trunk, though, and now I'd like to be very far away from this motel."

So would I, except I have no idea where to go or how to get there. And I'm tired. So tired that I could almost forget how scared I am.

"Where did your friend go?"

Malcolm's swollen eye twitches and I feel a flicker of pity, but I quickly shake it off.

"Okay, that's the first thing we need to get straight. That guy back there?" He points over his shoulder. "We don't work together. The first time I saw him was when he came busting down my door and proceeded to kick the crap out of me and toss me into the trunk of my own car when I wouldn't answer his questions fast enough."

"Any why would he do that if you're so innocent?"

Malcolm leans back against the wall and slowly sits. "I never said I was innocent, but I'm just the computer guy. I never hurt anybody, and I took this job with the understanding that no one else would get hurt."

I scowled. "Except me and my mom, you mean."

"No." He straightens so suddenly that he winces. "Look, no one even knew *you* existed until a few days ago. The cops have been looking for your mom for nearly two decades. Most people thought she was dead until she showed up at Derek's grave."

My entire body threatens to go limp with relief. "Then you've got the wrong person. You don't know her, but she barely lets me out of her sight, even to go to school. I always know where she is, and the only grave she's ever visited is the one we've been to together: my dad's. You've got the wrong person."

Malcolm doesn't try to argue; if anything, he looks sorry for me. "Two months ago, your mom didn't take a little road trip to Pennsylvania? Maybe you went with her but she slipped away for an hour or two?"

I open my mouth to deny it, but the words get stuck. We did go to Pennsylvania after our hiking trip at the end of summer. Mom's in love with this pie stand in Perkasie, a little town about thirty miles north of Philadelphia, whose name literally means "where hickory nuts were cracked." We make the drive every few months, staying the weekend in various B&Bs, and it's about the only time that Mom lets me go off on my own without first giving her a detailed itinerary of where I'll be at every moment of the day. I get a few hours to myself to do a little shopping, soak up the sun if the weather is nice, or even go ice-skating if it's during the winter. But Mom is always in our room with a book, waiting for me, when I get back. She would have told me if she went somewhere. I would have known.

My mouth closes.

"The police had a theory. They said Derek's death was a crime of passion, and because of that, his killer might feel safe enough to visit his grave after several years," Malcolm says. "They monitored the cemetery at first but eventually moved on. Then this year, Mrs. Abbott hired a private investigator, and he interviewed the staff. They confirmed that no one apart from family ever visits Derek's grave, but that a woman has been visiting the grave beside his every few months for a decade."

A decade. My brain scrambles to try and remember how long we'd been going to Perkasie. Can it have been ten years? Is that why all our frequent moves have never taken us away from the East Coast? So Mom could stay within driving distance of Derek's grave?

Malcolm continues, softer this time, and his words feel like spiders on my skin.

"The investigator set up a motion-activated camera near the grave, and he got a hit two months ago when the woman visited. She stayed for an hour, and right before she left, she reached out her hand to brush Derek's tombstone. He got a picture of her face when she left, and I was hired to try and match it with a photo online to locate her. I set up my facial-recognition program and eventually got a hit when the picture of the two of you was uploaded to the dating site. It was the same woman from the cemetery. Your mom *is* Tiffany Jablonski."

I'm sitting down. I don't remember when my legs refused to hold me up anymore, but I'm on the ground and the chill of the earth is seeping through my jeans and causing goose bumps to break out all over my skin.

It's just the cold, I tell myself. *Not anything else. Not these lies that can't possibly be true.*

I think about my mom: the way she traps daddy longlegs under glasses to set them free outside, the way she leaves notes in my lunch every morning and cries over commercials with puppies in them. She could never kill someone. Maybe she did know Derek Abbott, and if she's been secretly visiting his grave for years, then she obviously cared about him. Maybe she was a witness and was too scared to come forward. That would be the kind of mistake that could haunt a person. Or maybe her mistake was something else entirely.

Nothing that Malcolm has said proves she played a role in his death.

"I can't believe she killed someone. I just can't." I lift my gaze to his. "If you were me, you wouldn't believe it either." I'm chewing my lip, considering my options, when, out of the corner of my eye, I see Malcolm gingerly pushing to his feet. In less time than it takes to blink, I have my knife in my hand. His light-brown eyes slowly bounce from the weapon to my face and back again.

"Really?" he says, taking a careful step toward me. "My lightning-quick leap to my feet prompted you to get all stabby?"

I tighten my grip, but he doesn't seem intimidated at all.

Holding his side, Malcolm limps closer, until he can see into the parking lot, where the manager is still struggling to wrestle the door to my old room back into place. "Think that'll take him another five minutes?"

"Why?"

"Because I need that reward money, and the only way I'm going to find your mom again is if you help me, which you're not going to do unless I can prove I'm telling the truth. So I'm going to get you to someone you can believe."

LOOKOUT

I'm playing lookout.

Malcolm and I are inside the motel office. He's hunched over the computer while I chew my lip and peer outside at the manager unscrewing the busted hinges on the door to room 5.

"Here," Malcolm calls, backing away from the desk and motioning me over.

When I join him, I see a video cued up of a reporter standing in front of a run-down metal Airstream surrounded by other similarly neglected trailers. Malcolm taps a key, and the pretty woman with deep-bronze skin, gleaming white teeth, and black hair starts talking.

"Coworkers say seventeen-year-old Tiffany Jablonski took an instant and obsessive interest in Derek Abbott when he started coming into the coffee shop where she worked. They say she wouldn't let anyone else take his orders, and she wrote increasingly inappropriate messages on his cups."

Mom is young in the school photo on the screen, probably around my age. She looks dim somehow, sad. In contrast, the photo of Derek Abbott is a vibrant, laughing candid of him sailing. He's handsome, with sun-kissed hair and skin. The reporter shows more photos of him, describing him as warm and friendly, painting a portrait of a young man with a bright future cut tragically short.

"Derek's parents told police the infatuated teenager didn't take it well when their son failed to return her feelings. They say she broke into his family's house one night when he was there having dinner, and was found waiting for Derek upstairs in his old room—in his bed." Footage is shown of the grand Abbott estate, where the incident took place. "Derek asked her to leave, and she refused. His parents threatened to call the police, and she grew enraged, demanding that Derek admit he invited her there. When he denied it and tried to move her away from his parents, she attacked him and pushed him down the stairs. The coroner's report says he died instantly. Tiffany Jablonski fled the scene."

My stomach bottoms out, and I'm ready to click the video off when it cuts back to a live shot of the reporter standing in front of the Airstream, identified as Mom's childhood home. The door bangs open, and a man with shaggy gray hair and deep bags under his eyes emerges.

"Get the hell off my property!"

The reporter's eyes light up, and she pushes her microphone

73

into his face. "Mr. Jablonski, did you know your daughter was obsessed with Derek Abbott?"

My fingers rise up to cover my mouth. That's my grandfather. He died just before I was born, so I've never even seen a picture of him. Mom always said there was nothing about her childhood she wanted to remember. But now he's right there. Or he was, I remind myself. For a moment, I feel an ache because I never knew him, but I shove it aside.

He makes a failed grab for the reporter's microphone, but she nimbly dodges him and returns it to his face.

"Have you been in contact with her since the night Derek died?"

"She didn't do anything wrong. You condemned her because some rich boy's family pointed a finger. You can rot in hell, every last one of you."

"So you didn't think it was wrong for her to—"

"Seen enough?" Malcolm's arm reaches around me to stop the video.

"What? No. That's my grandfather. He doesn't think she killed him. He—"

But Malcolm has already closed the browser, and a few keystrokes later, the check-in software is back on the screen. I'm pushing to get back in front of the computer when the bell above the front door chimes and the disgruntled manager walks back in with his toolbox. He halts when he sees us behind the desk.

"Hey, you can't be back there," he says, a slight waver in his voice betraying his unease.

In a flash, I remember the easy smile Mom slapped on for Mr. Guillory, and I quickly hitch one onto my own face. "Oh, I'm sorry. There was no one here, so we were just looking around in case there was a note on the computer or something." I might have been able to sell that story if I'd been alone, but with Malcolm's face looking like he just went twelve rounds with a battering ram, beads of sweat begin to dot the manager's bald head, and his feet shuffle ever so slightly backward.

I shift so that my torn jeans and cut hip are facing away. Then, impulsively, I lean into Malcolm, linking my arms around his waist. I feel him wince. "Jake is an amateur boxer, welterweight, and believe it or not, he actually won tonight." I brighten my smile at the manager.

Malcolm slings his arm over my shoulder and drops a kiss on my forehead. "Baby, with you, I always win."

My smile falters for a split second when his lips touch my skin, reminding me of Aiden. Aiden, who has no idea where I am—because of Malcolm. I want to fling away, to grab for my knife and make a threat I could actually follow through on. Instead, I force my smile back to its full wattage and pray that the manager buys our story, that he can't see how tightly I'm gritting my teeth.

The manager's gaze darts between us a couple more times

before his shoulders relax and he sighs. "I don't give discounts. I don't care what you won. Now get out from behind my desk."

We move quickly, and I'm careful to still keep my hip facing away.

"Rooms are sixty-five dollars."

Before I can think of something to say, Malcolm leans forward and lowers his voice. "Hey, man, you sure about that discount? 'Cause I've only got fifty on me right now."

With a flat expression, the manager invites us to get out.

⌇

I make good on my earlier desire to fling myself away from Malcolm the second we're out of sight. And it's only the ashen color that sweeps over his face from the abrupt movement that keeps me from pulling out my weapon.

"Don't do that again," I say.

He's panting a little and leans some of his weight on a nearby car. "Do what? Follow the act you started and convince that guy not to call the cops?"

"Would that have been so terrible? You're not tied up anymore. *I* wouldn't have to explain anything. *You* would." I realize for the first time that I don't need a weapon to scare him. I don't even need the threat of his coworker, the bounty hunter, finding him again. "Why haven't you told me to call the police? If all you care about is bringing a killer"—I trip a little over the word but push on—"to justice, then why wasn't that the first thing you said?"

He's glaring at me, and it takes him a moment to smooth the expression from his face. "Calling the police is just going to bring a whole lot more heat down on your mom."

The frigid air hasn't thawed in the slightest, but the cold that had been seeping into my bones recedes a little. "And you suddenly care about me and my mom, is that it? What exactly were you hired to do, and how much are you getting paid to do it?"

"Nothing if it doesn't lead to your mom." He swallows before continuing, his reluctance clear. "Finding your mom through conventional methods failed for nearly twenty years. I was hired to try unconventional ones."

"You mean illegal ones."

He doesn't deny it. "I did what I had to do."

Disgust ripples over me. "What happened to you, getting beaten and tied up, that's what could have happened to my mom and me if we hadn't gotten away—or worse. That's what could still happen to my mom." I will not let myself think that something like that has already happened to her. "All that so you could, what, pay off some student loans? Buy a car with a trunk that opens from the inside next time?"

Narrowing his eyes, he reaches into his back pocket, and I leap back until I see it's only his wallet he grabbed. I instinctively catch it when he tosses it to me.

"Open it."

The leather is buttery smooth in my hands. Inside, I find his driver's license, his Penn State student ID, a handful of other cards, and tons of concert ticket stubs. But I also find pictures, dozens of them, all featuring the same older woman with Malcolm's dark skin and deep-set eyes. He's in a lot of the photos with her. In one, he's blowing out five candles on a homemade birthday cake the woman is holding, and in another, he's standing in a cap and gown while the much-frailer-looking woman beams up at him. The most recent photo is of him planting a kiss on her cheek as she lies in what is clearly a hospital bed.

"That's Gran. She took me in when I was six. She's the reason I'm in college. When she got sick, I lost my scholarship, taking care of her, and when she needed more, I took a job to find a woman accused of killing someone, and I made damn sure I found her."

He's still glaring at me, almost daring me to find fault with his motives. "You think I would have signed on if I knew I was gonna end up in a trunk, probably on my way to a shallow grave somewhere?"

"But you were fine securing that fate for my mom and me? Ignorance is not the same as innocence."

He grits his teeth. "No, are you even listening? I didn't know about you. I didn't know anything about your mom beyond what I read in the police report or found online. A name and some pictures, a bunch of random facts, and that's it." He waits for me to lean back and slow my breathing. "I was supposed to send a notification when I found her, but I hesitated when I"—he pauses—"found out about *you*. And that's when our friend showed up at my place, threatening to kick my teeth in if I didn't give him everything I had. . . ." His voice fades. "You and your mom were gone when we got to your house. He dragged me in with him, thought I could find something on your computer. I didn't. I wouldn't even go in your room, so he grabbed it for me."

That's when I realize he thinks he's giving me an excuse, something that exonerates him.

"So you just waited in the hall while he ransacked my room and brought you my laptop? I guess that gave you just enough time to steal that photo of me and my mom I found in your pocket."

"I wasn't thinking. I just . . . didn't want him to have it."

My voice is ice-cold. "You led him to the motel."

"He would have killed me if I hadn't. I hacked into traffic and security cameras, and it took a couple days, but there are only so many places to hide."

"And my mom? Did you tell him where to find her too?"

He shakes his head, his eyes so close to mine. "I don't know where she is. I thought she was here with you. That's the truth."

The problem isn't that I think he's lying to me anymore. I believe him. And if he doesn't know where my mom is, then I don't know what I'm supposed to do.

"Could you find her, like you found me?"

"Honestly? The only reason she was found this time is—"

"Because of me. I'm the one who created the dating profile for her and uploaded that photo." I blink away the sting in my eyes when I feel Malcolm's gaze, but he doesn't look away.

"What?" I say.

"I wasn't lying. The news story told you the same thing I did."

No, he wasn't, but parroting a story doesn't make it true, and my expression says as much.

Flinging his arms out as much as his cracked-if-not-broken ribs will allow, Malcolm says, "Then what? That's all I've got." He gestures back toward the office. "I tell you the truth. You don't want it, which, hey, I get—it's not a good truth. So I give you news footage saying the exact same thing and you still don't want it. And that wasn't even an old story, that's from like five years ago and it hasn't changed. It's not gonna change, so—" His voice chokes off as I step right into him.

"Five years ago? Are you sure?"

"Yeahhh." He draws the word out and tries to move back, but I'm literally crowding him.

I don't even care that this means my mom lied to me again. Because I know what to do now.

My grandfather didn't die before I was born.

And Malcolm is going to help me find him.

80

RECRUIT

When I tell him my plan, Malcolm laughs.

"Yeah, right." When I don't laugh back, his brows draw together. "Do you have a death wish? Look at my face. This is what will happen if we're caught. What, you think the bounty hunter'll take it easier on you 'cause you're a girl? He'll do whatever he has to in order find your mom and get his hundred grand."

"A hundred thousand dollars?" My knees go a little weak. "That's how much Mrs. Abbott is paying for my mom?"

Malcolm side-eyes me. "She's been waiting for decades to find her son's killer."

My spine snaps tight. "Stop calling her that. You were right there. You heard my grandfather. He doesn't think she did it, and he knew her better than any of those other people."

"It's called denial."

"No, it's called doubt, as in what I have about you. If you

81

weren't so obsessed with claiming your reward money, you'd be questioning this too." For the first time since finding him in the trunk, I turn my back on Malcolm. I'm not afraid of him anymore, and I feel like it has to be an insult to show him that. I bite both my lips, trying to distract myself from the ache in my chest. I face him again. "What I *want* is to talk to my mom, to hear the truth from her, but I can't do that. You just confirmed that the only other person who thinks she's innocent is still alive. And all that research you did trying to find my mom? You know where he is, don't you?"

Malcolm stares at me and swears under his breath. "He lives in a retirement facility outside Philadelphia, a *heavily surveilled* retirement facility. Plus the staff would have been given instructions to call the investigator if anybody so much as gets near him. And, in turn, the call would go out to people like our steel-toed-boot-wearing friend. Wanna guess what happens if you show up? And if I'm with you? I'm betting I bypass the trunk entirely. So, no. Go ahead and pick up your weapon and ask me again."

I was holding the makeshift knife again, but as a reflex, not as a means of intimidation. Despite his confidence, his eyes are darting slightly, like when we hid under the bed. He's not incredulous; he's terrified. "Think about—"

"Oh, I have. See, there's not much else to do when you're tied up in a trunk for days on end. I know exactly what I'm going to do. The way I see it, your mom is going to come back for you as soon as she thinks it's safe. As long as I stick by you,

I'll be right there when she does, ready to make that call, get my money, move my gran into the best place possible, and forget that any of you ever existed. That's *my* plan. *Your* plan . . ." His eyebrows climb nearly all the way to his hairline. "*Any* plan where I voluntarily go near people like that bounty hunter can go to hell."

"But that's just it," I say. "It's never going to be safe. *I'll* never be safe with her if she's the one people are hunting. She knows that. That's why she left, and it's why she's not coming back." My voice goes hollow as the truth of my words pierce through me. For days, I've been tormenting myself with scenarios where she was hurt, attacked, desperate to get to me but couldn't. The truth is somehow worse.

She was never going to call me.

She was never coming back for me.

As long as she's wanted in the death of Derek Abbott, she has to run, even from me.

"Then screw it." Malcolm spits the words out. "I'm sorry about your life and all, but I didn't do this. You can do whatever you want, Katelyn Reed, or Jablonski, or whoever you are, but I'm not dying for a hundred grand. I'm out."

I catch his wrist just as he starts to turn away, panicked at losing this last chance, this only chance, of finding my mom. Because I have to find her, now that I'm certain she's not going to find me. I drive steel into my voice and lock my fingers tight. "It's too late for that."

He snaps his eyes from my hand to my face, and in a low,

calm voice, says, "Let go, or I'll make you." His expression alone would have had me recoiling if my mom's life weren't on the line. I tighten my grip. I don't know why his fear relieves me of mine, but it does.

I drop the knife on the ground and then wipe my clammy hand on my pants. "Your name is Malcolm Pike. You're a sophomore at Penn State, you love your grandmother, you drive a navy Honda Accord, and judging from all the ticket stubs in your car, you really like some band named Laughing Gravy." I watch my fingers curling around the ripped denim of my jeans, instead of watching him. "The only other thing I know about you is that you effectively ended my life with a single keystroke. Maybe you're innocent, or maybe you're just a really good liar and you knew exactly what was going to happen to my mom and me. Either way, it's all the same." I force my hand still and look at him. When Malcolm's expression doesn't even flicker, I push home.

"The guy who hurt you and tied you up, what's gonna happen when he opens your trunk and finds you gone?" Malcolm's arm jerks in my hand. "Will he forget it and let you go back to your life? Will you be able to talk your way out of it once he kicks down your door? Will he believe it's a coincidence that I escaped at the exact same time as you?" I let my eyes drift over his injured side. "Or will he have to crack a few more ribs until you explain that I took you hostage? Here." I kick the knife toward him. "You can use this to sell your story.

He might even split the money with you if you manage to find my mom again."

I feel the pressure building up behind my eyes. I hate the way I'm putting every ounce of strength into holding his wrist. I hate that I'm afraid it won't be enough, that he'll fling me off and leave me utterly alone. But I need him, and if being scared and angry is the way to keep him, then so be it.

"Right now, we're running from the same person. And if you want me to even consider that my mom was involved in Derek's death, then I need you to take me to my grandfather. You need me to get to my mom and your reward money. You said it yourself that I'm the only reason you found her this time. If that's true, you need me just as much as I need you. You can't say you didn't do this. If it helps you sleep better, you can say you didn't *mean* to do this, but you're still responsible. You're involved. And you don't get to run away from it. You can be a coward after I get to talk to my grandfather."

He whispers one derisive word under his breath, never taking his eyes off me.

But he stops trying to walk away.

STEAL

Okay.

I know what I need to do. Find my grandfather and find out why he's so convinced that Mom is innocent.

I have Malcolm, who not only knows exactly where my grandfather is but also knows how to get past a security setup.

It's a start. And right now a start, a direction, is all I need. I'm tired of running from what I don't know.

But the problems with my plan begin to mount almost as soon as Malcolm stops trying to walk away.

Namely, he can't walk. Not well, at any rate, and definitely not far. Plus walking to my grandfather—who lives in Cheltenham, Pennsylvania—is not an option. I don't know where Mom drove us, but as far as she could get us in a night is a safe bet.

"Columbus, Ohio," Malcolm says when I ask.

Okay.

That's not too bad. It may be two states away from our home in Bridgeton, New Jersey, but it's only one from my grandfather.

And if my mom could drive it in one night, so can I.

I just need a car.

I don't have a car. Malcolm doesn't have a car. Or he does, but not currently. I also don't have enough money. Mom left with whatever money she may have had. I've got maybe twenty bucks on me, and Malcolm doesn't even have the fifty he tried to bluff the motel manager with, a fact he almost cheerfully informs me of when I ask.

Aiden has a beat-up Dodge Ram that could probably plow straight through the woods behind us, along with anything else that got in its way. Right now, he thinks I stood him up, ghosted him, but he'd still answer if I called. And he'd come. Even if I told him it was dangerous, he'd try to help.

Because he's a good guy. And he cares about me. Or he did. Maybe he hates me a little bit right now, but he'd still come if I needed help.

And I care about him too much to even consider letting him.

Mom thought she'd stashed me somewhere safe, at the motel, and they found me. If these people found our home, then they can find our friends. Better they hate me than get hurt because of me.

"We'll just have to pawn something," I say, seizing the faint memory of passing a pawnshop not too far down the road.

"Yeah, and what's that? My bloody hoodie or your torn jeans?"

"You don't have anything?"

He raises an eyebrow. "You didn't find my diamonds when you frisked me before? I always keep some on me." He starts patting his pockets, an exaggerated frown on his face.

I don't have the energy for this. Of course he doesn't have anything of value on him. He was bound and gagged in a trunk for as many days as I was pacing my motel room.

"What about *that*?" Malcolm nods at the chain around my neck, and the ring hidden beneath my shirt, which I'd been unknowingly clutching. I tighten my hold.

"No."

"What is it?"

"It's the ring my dad proposed to my mom with, and it's fake anyway, so . . ." It might be fake in the sense that it's costume jewelry, but it's worth more than any real diamond ever would be to me.

"I didn't have time to find out anything about him, but you said he's dead? Any chance your mom lied about that too?"

I shake my head. I was at the funeral. I was little, only four, but I remember the scratchy stockings I had to wear, and that

Mom didn't cry until we got back home, when I found her sobbing on the kitchen floor over the ring I now clutched. We cried together.

Vivid memories crash over me, sapping what little energy I have left.

"You think this part is hard? Wait till we have to sneak into a building that I can guarantee has papered its walls with your picture by now," Malcolm says.

Every part has been hard. Every. Part. I'm flirting with a complete mental and physical breakdown. Fear is the only thing driving my body, and my brain is ready to surrender control. I'm already thinking how easy it would be to slide to the ground and hug my knees and shut down.

But I can't do that. Not yet.

I suck in a deep breath.

Money.

Car.

Grandfather.

Answers.

I just need to think. I can do this. I have to do this. Malcolm pushes the hood off his head, and my eyes catch on the drawstring.

That could work.

I grab one end and pull the string free. It's nearly as long as my outstretched arms. I loop it around two of my fingers and tie a slipknot in the middle.

"What are you doing?"

"Getting us a car." It never ceased to amaze me how often Mom locked her keys in the car. After her third hour-long wait for a locksmith, and Mom watching carefully each time the car was unlocked, she figured out a few tricks and passed them along to me. Then Mom would randomly—though now I suspect not so randomly—lock her keys in the car and leave it to me to get us back in.

I hadn't tried this particular method with a hoodie string before, but the principle is the same. I just need to find an older car with a pop-up lock, work the string with the slipknot under the edge of the doorframe, and saw it back and forth until the loop hovers over the extended lock inside. Then I'll pull both ends of the string, cinching the loop tight, and yank up.

Easy.

Except I still haven't moved; I can't believe I'm considering stealing a car.

"Seriously?"

My gaze snaps away from the cars in the parking lot to lock on Malcolm. "I don't have a better idea and I don't have time to think of one, so yes."

Then Malcolm is muttering something to himself and abruptly toes off one of his sneakers.

I see it immediately. A thick stack of folded bills.

CONFESS

It's close to three thousand dollars. And he had it in his shoe.

My gaze drifts up from the bills to his face. "Seriously?"

"What—you want to complain now?"

No, I don't. But who walks around on that much money? Like he's *literally* walking around on it. "What if the bounty hunter had found it?"

"Then that would have sucked for me slightly more than this." He shoves the cash into his pocket and turns in the direction I indicated, since we're both eager to leave the motel far, far behind us.

I follow, and it takes an agonizingly long time to shuffle-walk with Malcolm to the little strip mall down the street. I keep throwing sidelong glances at him.

"What?" he asks through gritted teeth, and I can't tell if it's more the pain from his side or what I'm forcing him to do that earned me that irritable response.

91

"What do you have against banks?"

He doesn't answer.

The pawnshop has long since closed, not that we need it anymore, but we do find a surprisingly kind man at the gas station nearby, who's much more taken with our boxer story than the motel manager was, and lets me use his phone to hop on Craigslist, find the cheapest running car possible, and give the seller the address to meet us.

The car is . . . a car, so I don't care that it looks like something that barely survived a monster truck rally, or that the floor is rusted clear through in places so that I can see the road passing beneath us.

Malcolm, on the other hand, cares slightly more, given that the owner had sensed our desperation even before he saw us in person and claimed multiple other offers to jack up the price. In the end, it takes nearly all of Malcolm's cash to buy it. We have enough left for gas and the few other necessities that we need for the journey, but not a lot else. I don't worry too much until a few hours later, when Malcolm takes a deserted side road and eases the car onto the shoulder.

I jerk forward and clutch the dash. "What are you doing? I didn't tell you to stop."

Malcolm shifts into park. "My ribs are on fire. I need to take a break." He eyes the sharpened piece of window ledge I'm still holding. "You are still well within stabbing range, okay?" His eyes flutter closed as he unbuckles his seat belt and winces. "I'm not saying you didn't do a good job of being threatening back at the motel, but enough. You need my help, and you've made sure I need yours." He hisses in a breath and reclines his seat, then lifts his hoodie. I blanch.

Even against his dark skin, I can see the deep bruising wrapping around his ribs and muscled torso. No wonder he had trouble moving; I'm amazed he's been able to sit up and drive as long as he has. I stare at him a second longer, then reach into the backseat for the bottle of painkillers. I toss it at him, along with an extra water bottle. He knocks back way too many pills, and it's strange that after being chased and abandoned and fleeing for my life through the woods, I can still feel sympathetic for someone who literally caused this mess.

He hands the bottle back.

"How much farther?" I say.

"Four or five hours."

"Can you make that?"

Malcolm doesn't even open his eyes as he answers. "Yes, but I need to sleep. And so do you."

The weight of my eyelids is becoming unbearable, unconsciousness beckoning me like the sweetest lullaby. I do need to sleep. My brain feels like it's full of cotton, and even the simplest decision is beyond me. I hurt all over too: my head, from smashing into both the window with Mom and the pavement at the motel; my hips, hands, and knees, from falling out the window; my ribs, from Malcolm kicking me. We need to lie down somewhere that won't have us panicking at the slightest sound.

But I force my eyes open wide. I'd let them close once while Malcolm was driving and almost immediately had a vision of Mom with bruises like his. I can't sleep if it means seeing that again. "Then I'll drive. I don't think I can sleep."

He stops my hand when I reach for the keys and shakes his head.

"We can't go in until afternoon anyway, so we either kill time now while it's dark and no one's around or we hole up somewhere during the day, when someone is much more likely to notice us."

"Why afternoon?"

Malcolm's eyes have drifted shut again. "Can't you just trust that I know what I'm doing here? I've got a hundred thousand reasons to want this to work."

If I had the energy, I'd laugh. "It doesn't seem like you need the money, based on what you were keeping in your shoe."

"That was every dime I had to my name. This"—he gestures at the rusted-out car—"is not what I was going to spend it on."

A fresh wave of weariness washes over me. "Enough okay? I'm not going to feel sorry for you. You got into this with both eyes open, and I'm the last person you want to be complaining to. So stop."

I'm actually surprised when he does.

After a few minutes of silence, I glance over to find his eyes still open and his frowning gaze trained out the window. When

I hear his stomach growl, I pass him some of the protein bars before grabbing two for myself. I watch as he inhales three of them before I've finished my first.

Right. He's been in a trunk. I offer him another bar, and he takes it.

"We have to wait because there's a shift change at five. Employees in, employees out. Plus visiting hours end at six, so there will be a lot of unknown people to keep track of."

An actual answer. And it makes sense. I nod and look back at the things we bought and still need to use: hair dye, scissors, a razor, clothes. And makeup—most of which is for him so we can try and hide the damage done to his face. "We'll just slip in?"

"Something like that."

"So tell me. I need to know exactly—"

"No, you don't. You *want* to know. There's a difference."

Irritation tightens my lips. "Just because I'm not holding a knife on you anymore doesn't mean I'm not in charge."

"Actually, that's exactly what it means." Malcolm crumples up the wrappers and tosses the empty water bottles into the backseat before pushing his door open.

Panic courses through me, and I'm ready to lunge for him when he announces that he's just going to pee.

I went at the gas station, but Malcolm was done with walking by then and opted out. Still, I find myself counting the seconds until he returns.

Malcolm studies me warily when he settles against his seat and reclines it as far as it'll go. After a minute of watching me jump at the slightest noise, he hits the recline lever of my seat, and the back drops out behind me. I'm reaching for the blade in an instant.

"You're making my ribs hurt just from watching you. Worry tomorrow. Relax tonight."

"I can't relax." The muscles in my neck tense as I speak. I don't want to list all the reasons why, but that doesn't stop them from zipping through my mind again and again and again.

"You're different than I thought you'd be," Malcolm says, eyeing the blade that I have to force myself to set down again. "The girl in the picture looked less homicidal."

"The girl in the picture wasn't being hunted. But you took care of that."

He doesn't seem offended by the accusation. "If it wasn't me, it would have been someone else."

"So why was it you?"

Malcolm smiles, one corner of his mouth pulling to the side. "You ever hear of the Porch Pirate Punisher?"

"Should I have?"

He shrugs. "I guess it's mostly a Pennsylvania story." I'm beginning to think that Malcolm has a flair for the dramatic, because he makes me prompt him before he'll continue. "My dad was a hacker too. He's the one who taught me . . . a lot of things. Like not to trust banks, once he showed me how vulnerable they were. When I was younger, I thought he was kind of like Robin Hood, stealing from the rich and giving to the poor, you know? Except the rich were mostly regular people and the poor was always him—even once he had plenty of money." Malcolm shifts in his seat. "He went to prison for the first time for creating a software program that stole thousands of credit card numbers. He served two years, then was arrested again a few years later. See, he improved his program, made a few friends, and went from stealing and selling thousands of numbers to millions. He died from pancreatic cancer before being released, and I've been with my gran ever since."

"I'm sorry." It's an instinctual response to hearing about someone's loss, but I'm surprised to find I actually mean it.

"After he died, I decided I wanted to go the other way, use what I knew to help other people, not just myself. I rounded up a bunch of security footage from people who'd been robbed by porch pirates throughout the state of Pennsylvania, then I created a modified algorithm specifically to find their faces and ran it through every social media platform I could to identify them."

I can't help but smile. "That's cool."

"The FBI didn't think so. Though that was probably because I also coded a program based off the one my dad originally wrote to steal credit card numbers and then I posted the pirates' numbers online."

I gape at him. "You're lying. You'd be in jail."

A big self-satisfied grin stretches across his face. "Can't send a fifteen-year-old to jail. You can, however, scare the crap out of him by sending a bunch of feds to his school and yanking him out of homeroom."

"Wait, wait. That's not even possible. You said you identified porch pirates just from images you lifted off security cameras? At fifteen years old? I don't think so."

"Scary, isn't it? Granted my algorithm was in a league of its own, but there are programs, like Social Mapper and Find-Face, that can search through a billion photos from a normal computer in less than a second. Those two programs are much more basic and limited than what I created, but they do exist."

Something cold and painful lodges in my throat, like I'd just swallowed an ice cube. "That's why you were hired to find my mom, because of that program."

He nods. "I did gain a certain level of notoriety after that, but part of the deal I made with the FBI involved turning over my algorithm and everything else I had, with the understanding that I wouldn't get a second chance if I put on a black hat ever again."

"But you did."

He lifts one shoulder. "I had interest from a bunch of tech security companies when I graduated from high school, but my gran wanted me to go to college. And I wanted to prove to her that she could raise a good man. I ended up at Penn State in order to be close to her when she got sick. And when she got sicker, I took an offer that would pay me enough to take care of her."

We're both quiet after that.

After a few minutes, I open my door and throw my makeshift knife as far as I can into the tree line.

"Is that your way of telling me you want to be friends now?"

"No." I pull my door shut. "It just means I don't believe you're the bad guy anymore."

DISGUISE

I don't sleep, but Malcolm dozes on and off while we wait for dawn. When he's awake, we talk. Hearing his story and deciding to relinquish my weapon caused a shift between us. Despite my frequent attempts to get him to break down exactly what we'll be doing in order to get to my grandfather undetected, he keeps redirecting the conversation. He has no problem telling me things about him, though, and slowly I find myself opening up in return. I tell him about Mom's paranoia and strict parenting, along with the mostly successful ways I've gotten around her rules.

I even tell him about Aiden.

"You can't call him. You get that, right?"

I nod, but it doesn't make the thought of him hating me for disappearing on him any easier. I'd been telling myself to end it with Aiden for weeks, but I kept finding reasons—excuses, really—to hold off. Maybe he liked me more than I liked him, but it wouldn't have been hard to let myself go there.

And now . . .

"Maybe when this is all over, you can . . ." Malcolm doesn't finish. He needs my mom to be guilty, and either way, it's what he believes. If she's innocent, then he gets nothing. Worse than nothing, since he's already lost so much.

And if she's guilty and he can somehow convince me of that, then I'm supposed to . . . what, have a hand in sending her to jail?

Whatever happens, I'll never go back to our home in Bridgeton. But I hope I'll get to say goodbye to my friends and Aiden. To tell him . . . that he made me happy.

I wrap my arms around myself and squeeze, to push back against the ache rising in my chest, and that's when I notice that I can see the trees edged with reddish-gold light.

The sun is rising.

This early, traffic is practically nonexistent, so we're the only car at the next gas station we pull into. I tie Malcolm's hoodie around my waist to cover my hip, and request the bathroom key from the attendant inside. He gives me a concerned look, and I can feel his eyes on me as I go back out to where Malcolm is waiting. The two of us walk around the corner to the bathroom and squeeze inside.

As far as gas station bathrooms go . . . it's not the worst one I've seen, but I still have to breathe through my mouth. There's a toilet, a small sink, and one of those warped reflective metal domes that's supposed to act as a mirror.

With our backs to each other, we start stripping off our dirty and bloody clothes. I hiss when I have to peel the denim down my injured thigh. It's good that I saw Malcolm's torso the night before; the perspective allows me to examine my own scrapes and bruises somewhat detachedly. The cut on my hip doesn't look too hot. In a perfect world, I'd have gotten stitches; instead, I clean everything as best I can, then settle for a butterfly bandage and some gauze before carefully pulling on my new jeans.

I leave my old shirt on for the next part: dyeing my hair. Turning to grab the box, I notice that Malcolm is still trying to get out of his T-shirt, breathing slowly through his nose.

It's not going to happen. The best bet is to cut it off. I grab the scissors and slice straight up the back before pushing the ruined shirt off his shoulders.

"It looks better," I say. Better, in this case, means yellow and green streaks on his torso now, and the bluish and purple spots are smaller than before. And he's standing straighter, not leaning slightly to his left anymore. I'll make myself sick if I think about what he must have looked like on that first day.

"Yeah." He reaches for a wet paper towel. "Not sleeping in a trunk, five out of five doctors recommend it."

I pretend to search for something in his bag while he washes off the sweat, grime, and dried blood that clings to his skin.

He's visibly annoyed at needing my help when I face him again. I take the new T-shirt from his hand, bunch it up around the collar, and hold it up for his head to go through. I have to rise to my toes, because his injured ribs keep him from ducking. I think he tries to scowl at me, but it's a weak attempt.

Before helping him with the sleeves, I make another inspection of his ribs. I have no idea what visually distinguishes cracked ribs from broken ones, other than the fact that there are no obvious protrusions. I gently pass my fingers over his blotchy and bruised side.

He pulls back. "What are you doing?"

"Trying to tell if anything is broken."

"Since when are you a doctor?"

I drop my arms. "Since never, but if something is broken, then you'd probably need to go to a hospital."

"And where was your concern when you made me drive over here?"

"Waiting for an opportunity. This is it. Now turn sideways."

He stares me down for a good ten seconds before obeying. I try to be as gentle as possible, tracing each rib. His skin is hot under my fingers, and I'm not at all used to having my hands on a guy's bare chest. Even Aiden and I kissed only a handful of times.

That realization has me snatching my hands back, heat creeping up my cheeks.

I finish checking him quickly after that. Everything feels

fine, so far as I can discern. I think the most telling evidence is that Malcolm doesn't flinch away, though he does twitch a few times.

"What? I'm ticklish. Now if you're done groping me . . ." He tugs the T-shirt hanging from his neck.

When it's on, I toss his jeans at him. "You are doing your own pants."

That makes him smile.

Leaving him to that job, I pick up the scissors again and stare at the distorted reflection of myself in the metal above the sink.

Then I bend down to fish the photo of Mom and me from my backpack. In the picture, my auburn hair hangs long and loose, parted down the middle and rippling from the braids I'd slept in the night before. That's what I need my hair to not look like.

Lifting the scissors, I grab a section from over my shoulder and pull it taut between two fingers. It's the only way I've ever seen my hair: long, straight, and reddish brown.

I inhale and cut off a good eight inches.

Funny it doesn't hurt. It seems like it should. I take courage from that realization and chop off a new section, and then another, working my way around my head as best I can. I try not to look at the growing pile of hair at my feet as chunk after chunk falls to the floor. I take my time, not wanting it to look like I hacked away at my hair in moment of self-induced panic, even if that is close to the truth. The last thing I do is comb the front of my hair forward, over my face, and cut straight across at eye level. I hear the metal-glancing-over-metal rasp of the scissors, and I feel it in my teeth. I have no choice but to watch these new strands float down.

Malcolm slips the scissors from my hands and steps up behind me to even out the back. Our eyes meet in the mirror, and I'm very aware of how close we are. Even if I shut my eyes, I'd be able to feel the heat from his body. I shiver and grab the box of dark-brown hair dye I bought.

Apart from those spray-in colors at Halloween, I've never dyed my hair before. I read the directions three times before I slip the plastic gloves on and mix the dye. Then I close my eyes, lift the bottle to my hair, and squeeze.

The smell is a cross between rotten eggs and rotten eggs that have mated with the contents of a summer-ripe dumpster. The cut on my forehead, which trails back into my hairline, burns like I'm pouring acid on it, but I grit my teeth and keep going. The color looks much darker than it does on the box once it's all in: almost black. It would be upsetting if I were dyeing my hair for appearance's sake instead of camouflage.

Malcolm shaves while I wait, and I use the concealer we bought to cover his bruises. He looks younger than nineteen, and somehow more innocent, when we're done. When I first saw him tumbling out of the trunk, he'd been caked in blood and sweat, with several days' worth of stubble. He looked . . .

culpable. Now he looks like a college student, not a criminal. He looks like someone who prints out selfies with his grandmother, because he wants to have actual photos in his wallet.

Because that's who he is.

I think back to how I treated him and I want to apologize, but the words get stuck and then it's time to rinse my hair. Malcolm helps with this too, running his fingers up the base of my skull and using an empty water bottle to reach where the stubby faucet can't.

The dark rivulets that slither down the drain make my heart skitter, and I squeeze my eyes shut, scrubbing my hair until I'm sure the excess dye is gone. Every time I run my hands through the short strands, vertigo whirls through me.

My heart nearly stops for good when I catch my reflection for the first time, with hair that swishes at my shoulders instead of swinging beyond my lower back. The dark color makes my normally olive skin look wan and pale, and my eyes larger somehow. Peering through my new blunt bangs, I'm wary of the girl staring back at me. I look like I'm hiding. Or maybe that's just how I feel.

The bangs are too long to stay out of my eyes and too short to tuck behind my ears. They'll be constantly in my face, obscuring my features.

Okay. Okay. That's good. That's what I want.

Instead of fleeing outside, I confront my new appearance, getting as close to the mirror as the sink will allow. It's me, but not the me I've seen my entire life.

Malcolm half nods. "It looks good."

"I don't even recognize myself," I say, turning away from him while I change into my new shirt and jacket. "I guess that's the point, though."

He lowers his head, maybe to give me a semblance of privacy but maybe because he's the reason I can't afford to look like me anymore. I don't relish making him feel bad, the way I did just yesterday, but it's a good reminder all the same. He's not helping me out of the kindness of his heart; he's helping me because I forced his hand.

And we're hoping for radically different outcomes.

Eyes still cast down, Malcolm says, "I need to tell you something. That night you and your mom ran, I—"

Boom, boom, boom! A pounding fist. "Police. Open the door. Now!"

FORCE

Malcolm and I both jump, and I'm dimly aware of the way he shifts to place himself between the door and me.

"Just a minute!" I call. My adrenaline spikes as I throw myself to the floor and grab fistfuls of cut hair to toss in the toilet. Malcolm is right beside me, shoving our bloody clothes into our bags. I'm twisting around the small space, searching for anything we might have missed.

I know they'll hear the toilet flush and rightfully assume we're trying to hide something, but it can't be helped. More pounding on the door and issued commands, and my heart lurches painfully with each one; I can feel it trying to break free of my ribs. I place a hand on my chest. *I have to calm down. I have to calm down.*

Most of the hair is gone from the floor, and what's left could blend in with the general filth. Malcolm and I are dressed in clean clothes, and we've covered the worst of the bruises on his face.

Whatever this is, we'll talk our way out of it, just like with the motel manager.

I fling the door open and instantly squint at the sunlight that slaps me in the face.

"Step out of the bathroom."

I follow the officer's command, and I take Malcolm's hand to keep him by my side. I don't know if it's my imagination, but I think I see the officer's demeanor soften at the sight.

"Is there a problem?" I force my eyes open, and the bright sun makes them water. The officer is of average height but well above average weight, and I have the insane thought to just run. I don't think he'd be able to catch me. But could Malcolm run fast enough with his cracked ribs?

"Ma'am, are you all right?"

I nod quickly and tighten my hold on Malcolm's hand.

After staring at Malcolm for a long hard moment, the officer says, "The attendant told me he saw a man with a bloodstained sweatshirt enter the bathroom after you about forty-five minutes ago." His glance flicks to my wet hair before returning to Malcolm and the crisp white T-shirt he's wearing under an equally crisp hoodie. The officer's eyes snag at something where our hands are joined, and sweat prickles my neck as I spot a tag we forgot to remove.

"I'm sorry if we made someone wait." I shift forward to draw the officer's gaze back to me. "I wasn't feeling well and didn't want to be by myself in case I got faint." In the same movement, I push my new bangs to the side and rip the scab off my forehead to reveal what looks like a fresh cut. "We were in a car accident earlier, and I was worried I might have a concussion."

There's no indication from the officer that he believes me, and my hand in Malcolm's is growing slick.

"Where's your car?" the officer asks.

Automatically, I start to answer, my gaze sliding in the direction of where we parked down the street, but Malcolm beats me to it.

"We had it towed to a friend's house. The alignment was messed-up."

"And your friend didn't have a bathroom you could use?"

"He's not that good of a friend."

I swallow the flood of saliva filling my mouth as I watch Malcolm and the officer square off.

"But he lives close by? You wouldn't have made your girlfriend walk far if she has a concussion."

"He dropped us off," I say. "And anyway, I was overreacting. I'm feeling much better. We won't keep you." I start to pull Malcolm along, but the officer's words cut us off.

"I'd like to see some ID."

My fingers spasm around Malcolm's. "We don't have any on us."

"Do you have anything illegal in your bag?"

"No," I say, but my voice wavers.

"I'm going to need you to open your bags."

"Legally, we don't have to do that without a warrant," Malcolm says.

I turn toward him, surprised and more than a little impressed with the calm, even tone he's using.

The officer's eyes narrow, but a call comes through on the radio at his shoulder before he can answer. "You both stay right there." He retreats half a dozen steps and responds to the call.

"Is that true?" I whisper.

"Yes. My dad would have been arrested a lot sooner if he'd submitted to every search request he got. Without probable cause, the cops can't look in our bags."

"What about what the clerk saw? Doesn't that count?"

Malcolm doesn't answer right away, and I notice sweat beading on his upper lip.

"If he sees our bloody clothes . . ."

That would be bad, like questions-we-can't-answer bad, maybe handcuff-us-and-arrest-us bad. They'd find out who we are and who my mom is. *No, no, no. That can't happen.* I turn to Malcolm and pretend I'm leaning into him like a girlfriend. "Can you run?"

He keeps his gaze on the officer. "He's between us and the car."

Smiling like I don't have a care in the world, I drop my head on Malcolm's shoulder and add my free hand to the one already holding his. "I know."

He nods once, then again. "Leave the bags and start backing up."

Everything I have from home is stuffed in that backpack, but it'll slow me down if I try and keep it with me. I still have my dad's ring around my neck, and I brush it through the fabric of my jacket before lowering the bag to the ground. Malcolm does the same with the bag holding our supplies.

We take slow steps, shuffles really, and make it a few feet before the officer yells at us to stop.

Then we run.

PLAN

`Malcolm is fast.`

Fast like he must be lightning when he's not hurt. It takes everything I have to keep up with him, and though he constantly glances over—or back—to make sure I'm with him, he doesn't slow down until we're blocks and blocks from the police officer in pursuit.

We dart past cars, through parking lots and alleys, around dumpsters, and finally up and over a chain-link fence that Malcolm has to help me scale. I know when we jump down and he stumbles that his body is going to make him stop soon no matter how desperately his mind wants him to keep running.

The same impulse is still driving me: escape. But no one is chasing us, and Malcolm needs to stop. We're in a neighborhood now, and not running exactly, because neither of us wants to draw attention from anyone who might be looking out his or her window, but still moving quickly. I come alongside him and offer him my shoulder to lean on. We pass a detached garage with one of those swing-open doors, the kind that look like they belong on a barn, a simple lift latch at the base is all that's keeping it shut. I know it's technically illegal when I steer us toward it and we go inside, but we just ran from a cop, so it hardly seems to matter, especially since Malcolm is leaning more and more of his weight on me with each step.

No car. Hopefully, that means the owner is out driving it and not inside the house, calling 911 because he or she just saw two people breaking into their garage.

I tow Malcolm toward the back, past neatly stacked boxes and carefully stored furniture. It's the tidiest garage I've ever seen, and a pang of guilt hits me that we've broken into a place the owner takes such obvious pride in. I move a few boxes so we can sit, and when Malcolm drops onto one, I linger in front of him. "You okay?"

"I took a bunch of painkillers in the car, and they're starting to kick in. I just need to sit for a minute."

He sits for longer than a minute, eyes fixed on a box marked PAUL'S ROOM in thick black marker, the kind that squeaks when you use it. I love that kind.

"We should have taken turns in the bathroom," I say. "That way one of us would have noticed the clerk growing twitchy."

"It doesn't matter now," he says.

"We lost the car."

It goes without saying that neither of us is going to suggest heading back toward the cop to get it. By now, he's searched our bags, found our bloody clothes, and drawn whatever conclusions about them that he's going to. Will he call out a search for us? I have no idea, and I don't want to voice the question in case Malcolm does. Besides, he silently answers my unspoken question by growing visibly more agitated with every passing second. He starts darting his eyes all over the place and bouncing his knee incessantly.

"This is a bad idea," he says, and then looks at me. "We could both get caught. You get that, right?"

The box dips as I take a seat next to him. "That's true whether we go to my grandfather or not." More so after our run-in with the cop. The latest in my list of crimes. I'm supposed to be helping my mom and prove she's innocent, yet I was with her when we stole two cars and now I'm fleeing the police and breaking and entering, all while preparing to sneak past security in a retirement home.

"Yeah," Malcolm says, "but this is parking on the tracks and running toward the oncoming train when we should be sprinting like hell to get away from it."

Brushing the dark strands from my forehead, I prod the skin around the cut, and red smears my fingers. Unlike the time I saw my own blood in the Walgreens parking lot with Mom, my stomach doesn't violently empty itself on the spot. I don't know if I should consider that progress or proof that I'll never find my way back to the me I was before all this started.

I see a few towels folded on a shelf and take one. I'm now officially a thief, but I can't risk using my clean-if-slightly-sweaty shirt on the cut, and I definitely can't risk blood trickling down my face when we try and slip into the retirement home unnoticed. Malcolm doesn't have any open wounds, but I pass him the towel anyway and he uses it to mop the sweat off his face. "That's actually wrong," I say. "Statistically, your survival odds are better if you run toward the train, next to the tracks. When the train hits, it'll explode all the wreckage forward, likely impaling anything in front of it."

Malcolm wearily hands me back the towel, now stained with our sweat and blood. "Yeah, well, this is on the tracks."

"So you'd rather run blind? Forever?" Just saying those words makes my muscles cramp. I can't imagine living the rest of my life with these unanswered questions. Malcolm has much less at stake than I do, but hiding from the truth and being afraid like this every day until I die isn't a life I want to live, no matter what the risk.

"I'd rather not end up in another trunk."

"Me neither. And this is how we do that. Get information, track down my mom, and find out what really happened so we can run in the right direction. Now come on. What's the plan to get me in without getting caught?"

"Silver Living—that's the retirement facility where your grandfather lives—is about a mile from here. We can walk."

He'd said we were close when we stopped at the gas station,

but I hadn't realized we were *that* close. Something like excitement tingles inside me. Other than my mom, I've never met another member of my family before. "Okay. That's good," I say. Because I had no idea how we'd get another car if we were still miles and miles away. Although even as the thought passes through my mind, the answer chases right after it: I'd get a car any way I had to.

"And then what?"

I'd worried that Malcolm was lying about needing only a few minutes to rest, but the color is already coming back to his cheeks and his breathing is steadying.

"There are security cameras in every hallway, and we need a passcode and a key to enter each floor." He says this all dispassionately, but I feel my stomach clenching with every obstacle he lists.

"But you're a hacker. Can't you, you know, bypass all that?"

The look he gives me makes me feel utterly and completely stupid.

"I need access to a computer. There's probably an empty office somewhere inside, but it'll be locked."

I nod and nod again, like I'm calmly following along and not trying to keep the bile from crawling up my throat. "So we'll have to get someone's keys."

"Yeah," Malcolm says, but not like I came up with a solution, like I just exchanged one problem for another.

Keys. Mom got two sets of keys the night we ran. One by

conning our neighbor, and the second by means unknown. I'm feverishly wishing now that she'd explained exactly what she did inside the store that led to her leaving it with a stranger's keys in her hand.

"I need to be the one to get the keys," I say.

"What—why?"

"Because *you* look like you were in a fight." He's sweated off most of the makeup we used to conceal his cuts and bruises, and the towel has taken care of the rest. "Besides, you have to sneak into the office. Division of labor."

He rubs a hand over his face. "Do you actually know how to pick a pocket?"

"No, but I'll figure it out." I'm not giving myself another option.

HACK

"Oh, I'm so sorry," I say to the janitor who I just deliberately bumped into as he was exiting an office. "I'm supposed to be visiting with my grandmother, and I keep getting turned around." I add a tremor to my voice, and it isn't hard at all to call up a little moisture to my eyes, thinking about meeting my actual grandfather for the first time. "It'll break her heart if she thinks I didn't come." I shift around him so that he has to turn his back to the office door. "They told me she was having dinner, but I can't seem to find the dining hall. Could you show me?"

It takes everything I have not to stare at the door I need him to forget about locking. He has kind eyes, and I heard him whistling while cleaning the office. Surely he's the type to offer help to a visibly upset girl. . . . *Come on, come on.*

"I get lost all the time," he says with a wink, placing his keys atop his cart and offering me an elbow. "Let's go find that grandma of yours."

I glance over my shoulder as we round the corner, and see Malcolm grab the keys from the abandoned cart before sliding inside the office. A second later, the blinds all close, and I let out the breath I've been holding.

"Don't you worry," the janitor says. "Your grandma won't care if you're a few minutes late."

I make an excuse about needing to run to the bathroom once we get within sight of the dining hall. Then my hands go sweaty and I worry that I've overplayed my part when the janitor offers to pop inside and let my grandmother know I'm coming, if I point her out.

"That's so sweet, but I've already kept you too long. But thank you!" I dart into the bathroom before he can say anything else. I lean against the door as soon as it closes and wait until I hear the squeak of his sneakers retreating on the linoleum floor before slipping back out.

Malcolm said he needed only a couple minutes to hack into the CCTV footage and locate my grandfather. "They use Hikvision cameras," he said by way of explanation when I was skeptical about how much time he'd need. "A few years ago, a backdoor command line of code that granted admin level was discovered and exploited by hackers all over the world. Silver Living never bothered to update the firmware when the company released a patch, so, yeah, two minutes, tops."

He was so confident that I fully expected him to be waiting for me in the stairway we'd designated before splitting up, one ankle crossed over the other and leaning against the wall.

He wasn't.

Another minute passes.

Then another.

I'd made sure to keep the janitor away for a full five minutes by asking inane questions about every room we passed.

Five minutes plus two more at least. Probably closer to ten.

Maybe Malcolm oversold his skills.

Maybe the janitor returned, found Malcolm in the office, and called security.

Maybe Malcolm took the first opportunity he had to run and left me here alone without any idea how to find my grandfather.

Maybe he's already halfway down the street by now.

I chew the nails that haven't had a chance to grow since the last time I was left waiting for someone who never came back.

A door opens a couple floors above me, and a loud female voice floods the stairwell.

"That's what *I* said. But you know that old fool—he'd sooner bite me than smile. So I told him, 'Fine, George. I'll get you a comb for the one strand of hair you have left on your head.' So I go get him one and bring it back. And he takes one look at it, then at me, and says, 'Woman, why on God's green earth do I need a comb? You can see I'm bald as an eagle.'"

Another woman, one with a higher voice, laughs in response.

I press against the wall, trying to make myself as small and silent as possible. My heart beats faster, and even though a jittery pulse might help me sell my story again if those women come all the way down the stairs, the lie won't matter if Malcolm isn't there to tell me where to go once they're gone. I can't go up to the front desk and ask which room my grandfather is in. I can't even give the name of someone else on his floor, because I don't know anyone else.

And what if he did make it out of the office only to run into the bounty hunter or someone on Mrs. Abbott's payroll? Malcolm said they'd probably beefed up the surveillance after spotting Mom at the cemetery nearby—since, as far as they knew, her only other relative lived here.

I press a fist against my stomach, willing the acid to stop splashing around inside so I can think.

Think.

Think.

I leap a good foot off the floor when the door beside me swings open and Malcolm rushes in, panting.

"We have a problem."

DISCOVER

I stop worrying about the two women above us who are still chatting without seeming to even notice the hushed conversation between Malcolm and me.

"What exactly is the Memory Care Ward?" I ask. But I know, and what's left of my fingernails stab into my palms as my fists clench.

"He has dementia. Stage six, according to his chart. Once I found out where he was, I dug up his records. That's what took me so long." Malcolm takes in my fists and the way I'm biting my lip. He swallows, starts to reach out a hand to my arm, then rethinks the gesture. "He might not be able to tell you anything. You get that, right? There's only seven stages, so the odds—"

"It doesn't matter," I say, rounding on him and dimly registering the fact that my voice has raised enough for the woman above us to break off midsentence. When I reach for Malcolm's arm, I don't hesitate or second-guess the impulse. "He's the only one who knew her, who saw her and talked to her that day. There must be a reason he thinks she's innocent, and I need—" My voice cracks.

"Okay," Malcolm says. "Okay, then we'll try."

I could kiss him when he tells me that. I settle for hugging him and saying a thank-you that gets muffled in his shirt. When his arms come up around me, the memory of standing with Aiden as I tried to hurry him out my window jolts through me. At the time, I'd thought Aiden was brave, if slightly reckless, for taking precious seconds to hug me and even darting back to steal that last kiss. True, he'd been risking my mom's considerable wrath, but nothing more.

Malcolm snuck into Silver Living with me knowing full well what might happen if we were caught. And even now that we've just learned it might all be for nothing, he said okay when I insisted we go find my grandfather anyway.

He didn't have to do that.

I can feel his heartbeat. It's fast, and he's twitchy, scared, I realize, but still helping me.

I pull away, because if I can feel his heart, then he can feel mine. Whatever happens with my grandfather—and I'm still fiercely holding on to hope—if there's some way I can help Malcolm without betraying Mom, I vow right then that I'll find it.

Malcolm went above and beyond during those few minutes he spent in that office. Not only did he locate my grandfather's room and get the passcode to his floor, but he looped the camera footage in the hall outside. It doesn't matter who is monitoring the feed; they won't see anything as Malcolm pushes the door open for me and we step inside.

I see him right away, and it makes my breath catch and my chin quiver, because from the light pouring through the window he's sitting in front of, I can see that I look a little like him: it's the shape of our eyes, the slope of our noses. I want to laugh and cry and rush at him all at once. The only reason I don't is because he stares at me without any hint of recognition.

"Mr. Jablonski?"

His bushy gray brows pinch together. "I don't want to go to crafts, and I don't want to eat any more of that awful slop they serve in the cafeteria."

"Oh, no, we don't work here." I take a step toward him, and when he doesn't seem concerned by my proximity, I take another. "My name is Katelyn. Can I?" I gesture at the empty chair beside the lounger he's sitting in, and he gives me a gruff nod.

"And what does *he* want?" my grandfather asks, eyeing Malcolm.

"He's a friend of mine who gave me a ride. Um, Mr. Jablonski?" I wait for his narrowed gaze to leave Malcolm and return to me. I try not to be discouraged by the fact that it stays narrowed. "I was hoping to talk to you about your daughter."

"I don't have a daughter."

125

"But you do." I lean forward to snag the framed photo of Mom that I spot on his dresser. "See?" It's maybe the only personalized item in the entire room. I angle it toward him, and I can't stop myself from running a finger over Mom's smiling face. This is the photo they should have used in the news story. My mom can't be more than twelve in the picture, and she's sitting in the grass with a pair of sunglasses pushed back to flash a grin at the camera.

She looks happy.

She looks like my mom.

The frame is jerked from my hands. "Where is she? Where's Tiffany?"

"I-I don't know. I was hoping maybe you'd talked to her."

"Tiffany!" he yells. "Get in here right now!"

"No, no. She's not here. She had to go away—do you remember? It was a long time ago."

"Tiffany!" he calls again.

I cast Malcolm a panicked glance.

"Your daughter isn't here right now," Malcolm says in a low, calm voice. "But maybe we can help find her for you."

"Did you take her?" He surges to his feet, and there's the sound of shattering glass as the photo falls to the floor. "Where's my little girl?"

"No one took her," I say. "She left." I reach for his hand, bending low to grab the photo in the same movement. "She was accused of killing Derek Abbott."

"She never killed anyone."

126

My heart leaps as his gaze, seemingly clear for the first time, settles on mine.

"How do you know that?" I straighten up.

"She's just a little girl, my Tiffany." He pulls his hand free from my suddenly limp grip and takes the photo back. He knocks the remaining glass shards free with a knuckle and smiles at the picture. "Her mama was young too. Too young to look after Tiffany, so she brought her to me. What was I supposed to know about raising a little girl?" He shakes his head. "But she was so smart, and she didn't need anyone to raise her. Raised herself really." His smile slips. "I should have been better. I should have understood." Using his stubby fingers, he pries one corner of the picture free, then lifts the whole thing out. "I'd do it differently now. I wouldn't get so mad. Wouldn't yell at her and that boy." He angles the frame toward me and the dark, blurry image he's just revealed.

I don't understand what I'm seeing at first, the white hazy image and the matte-black background. Then I register the words printed in the corner.

It's a sonogram dated the week Derek died.

"She was pregnant." I whisper the words—not to anyone in particular, but Malcolm is suddenly right at my shoulder and staring, unblinking, at the image. "Was that in any of the news stories?" I ask him.

He shakes his head without looking away from the tiny little shape of the baby my mom carried before me.

But, no, that can't be right.

127

"Who was the father?" Malcolm asks my grandfather.

"My daughter isn't a whore," is the angry answer he's given. "Derek Abbott was the father."

Malcolm lifts his eyes to mine. "How old did you say you are?"

I feel like I've been plunged into ice water. "I'll be seventeen tomorrow."

Malcolm extends the sonogram to me. "Are you sure about that?"

"They're getting married," my grandfather says, oblivious to the earth-shattering implication Malcolm just made. "He told me himself when I found out about the baby. Gave her a ring and everything. Ugliest, flashiest thing I ever saw, but Tiffany wouldn't take it off, even though the thing must have weighed a good pound."

My hand is clutching the ring I've worn on a chain around my neck for as long as I can remember. Mom told me all about how my dad proposed after finding it at a flea market and how she never wore it because it was too gaudy. Looping my finger around the chain, I draw it out from beneath my shirt. In a weak, almost breathy voice I ask, "This ring?"

He lunges for me so fast that Malcolm has to dive between us.

"Thief!" he roars. "You stole my baby girl's ring! Thief! Thief!"

We can't get him to calm down, and even though his mind

might be impaired, his strength hasn't diminished. It's clearly taking everything Malcolm has to hold him back.

Cold needles into my bones as I try to get him to understand that I'm his granddaughter—Tiffany's daughter—and that she gave me this ring and told me it came from my father, who couldn't have been Derek Abbott. Derek died a year before I was born. And I knew my father; I have memories of him. Faint ones, but I have them. Mom didn't cry until he died, until that night I found her cradling this ring and lifting it off her neck to fasten around mine.

I'm not old enough. I'm turning seventeen. I'd have to be nearly eighteen if Derek was my father.

But staring at the face of the grandfather she'd told me was dead, the one who keeps calling her by the name she changed, it isn't hard to imagine her adding one more lie to the list: If she changed her name, why not change my age too?

Was it only after I was born that she met the man I remember as my father, the man who was kind to me and let me call him Daddy because of whatever sob story my mom invented for him?

Vomit begins burning its way up from my stomach, thawing the cold and scalding my throat.

My grandfather is still yelling—screaming, really—and I've stopped saying anything.

I hear footsteps pounding down the hall, and a second later the door opens.

SPLIT

Two people in scrubs rush past me and, misinterpreting the scene, one of them, a large man, bodily wrestles Malcolm away from my grandfather, while the other one, a slender woman with dense freckles all over her face, rounds on me.

"What are you doing here?" she says.

"Stealing from me!" My grandfather is straining to get past the male orderly who's trying to calm him down. "They took my daughter's ring!"

"We didn't. We—"

"You're not supposed to be in here," the woman says.

"I know. I'm sorry." My short hair whips around my face as I turn back and forth between her and my grandfather. "Is he going to be okay?"

The answer is an obvious no as he takes a swing at the male orderly, who has to lunge out of the way. The momentum from his missed punch sends my grandfather careening to the floor atop the shards of shattered glass.

I see blood as his forearms slice open, and feel my own blood drain from my face. Instinctively, I move to help him, but the woman blocks my way.

"You stay right there." Never taking her eyes from Malcolm and me, she lifts a bulky radio from her hip and calls for help. The other orderly bends over my grandfather, talking softly to him as he assesses the injuries.

"Who are you?" the woman says.

"We were . . . just . . . lost," I say, stammering a little.

Malcolm has been slowly edging his way around the room, and as soon as he reaches me, he says, "We'll go."

"Uh-uh." The woman's eyes sweep over my features until they still and widen.

And I know she knows.

Malcolm and I reach for each other's hands at the same instant.

"What are your names?" she asks, but there's a new inflection in her voice, one that tells me she doesn't need the answer.

"Amy," I say at the same time Malcolm says, "John."

We start backing up when the woman reaches for her phone instead of her Silver Living–branded radio. She moves slowly, as though she doesn't want to alarm us.

My grip tightens around Malcolm's hand, wanting to be wrong about the flicker of recognition I thought I saw in her face.

"This is Shannon Donnelly from Silver Living. I'm supposed to call this number if anyone visits Mr. Jablonski. Well,

I'm pretty sure I'm staring at the girl from the photo you just dropped off—"

Malcolm and I make a break for the door at the same time.

"No, the woman isn't with her. It's a young black guy. They just ran—"

That's all we hear before we burst out into the hall and collide with another orderly. All three of us go down. I feel my ankle twist, and have to bite back a cry. Malcolm lands hard on his side and isn't as successful at holding in a pained groan.

"I'm sorry, I'm sorry," I say to the fallen orderly, a slim, prematurely balding man, who looks stunned but not hurt. I grab Malcolm's arm and pull him to his feet.

Shannon bursts out of the room, nearly tripping over her fallen coworker. Her phone is still pressed to her ear. "Yes," she's saying as we sprint away as quickly as my ankle and Malcolm's ribs will allow. "I'm sure it's the daughter, but her hair is much shorter and darker now." I don't understand why she isn't chasing us until she adds, "Security is moving to cover the exits now."

We round one corner and dash down another hall. The building is huge and sprawling, and we didn't have the option of retracing our steps, so neither of us has any idea where we're going.

My ankle threatens to roll again as we skid to avoid an elderly woman pushing a walker. We pass more residents too, but only one other orderly, who calls out that there's no running in the building.

Every corner we round, every doorway we push through, I expect to see the bounty hunter waiting for us. Fear floods my system with adrenaline, and soon my body is slick with cold sweat. How close is he? When he lost Malcolm and me, did he come straight here, correctly assuming that I would too? What if he's been waiting right outside and Shannon's call sent him instantly charging in after us?

The heavy chlorine smell that clings to every surface is searing my lungs as I drag air in and out, and I start to feel like it's fogging my brain, clouding my judgment. I pull Malcolm into a random room and push the door shut behind us. Panting, he doesn't waste his breath with inane questions.

"We can't stay here," he says.

"We can't keep running blind down random hallways," I say, leaning against the door and pressing my fingers into the stitch in my side. "I'm pretty sure they eventually loop back to where we started."

Malcolm nods, then glances around. With more speed than either of us should have left in our reserves after the past twenty-four hours, he practically lunges at me and unceremoniously shoves me to the side to reveal a floor plan taped to the back of the door.

We silently scan the map and locate the nearest stairwell, which we'd somehow managed to plow right past. When I reach for the door handle, already bouncing on my toes, Malcolm grabs my wrist to stop me.

"I think we should split up."

He has to feel the tremor that pulses through me. I have been terrified almost nonstop for days. I'm hurt and exhausted, and it's taking every ounce of strength not to let waves of implications drown me, after what I just heard from my grandfather. And the only reason I'm able to do that is because Malcolm is right by my side—just as afraid, just as weary and with injuries far greater than mine.

I don't think I can keep it up alone. I know I can't. "No way. In together, out together. If we keep going a little farther, we—"

"We can't. By now the entire building is looking for two running teenagers. We need to walk, and we need to do it alone."

I hate the logic of his words. I hate it so much I start turning the doorknob anyway.

Releasing my wrist, Malcolm uses his shoulder to keep the door shut while he traces a path on the floor plan. "You can take the stairs down here, and I'll take the ones here." His finger slides inches to the right, past the office we infiltrated earlier. "A couple of hallways and we can meet up again here." His finger stops at the rear exit we entered through. "I'll be less than two minutes behind you. Then we can—"

"What about security?" I can't think beyond getting out of this building. I don't want to. Because once I'm outside, I have to confront things that I'm not ready to confront. Not now. Maybe not ever.

Malcolm makes a gesture halfway between a shrug and a

dismissal while finding the key I'll need and removing it from the ring. "Haven't you noticed how understaffed this place is? We've seen, what, four attendants on this entire floor? The lower floors aren't for people with cognitive issues, so my guess is they'll have even less. And if they can't afford staff, no way they can pay for legitimate security. At best, we're talking about a couple guys with radios, who I guarantee will be more scared of us than we are of them. If you see one, just run. If they're blocking a door, charge them." He's serious as he says it, still studying the map and frowning as he double-checks that he's picked the best routes.

"You want me to play chicken with a security guard?"

"If you have to, yeah. And here." He leans past me, so close that his cheek grazes my hair. He plucks a baseball cap off a hook on the wall and tugs it onto my head. He even tucks my hair behind my ears.

It sends a momentary trickle of warmth through me.

"I'm not stealing some guy's hat."

"Borrowing. You're *borrowing* some guy's hat. You can ditch it at the exit, and he'll get it back."

"What about you?" There aren't any other hats.

Malcolm grins at me, the first time I've seen him smile like he truly means it. "It wouldn't look nearly as good on me."

I decide to give in to an impulse then. It's not the first time I've felt it, and the timing is awful, but if I don't do it now . . . No, I mentally derail that thought before it can gather any real speed. There'll be lots of other opportunities. I'm doing this now because I want to. Because he's putting my safety ahead of his own. Because I don't want to think about anything else.

I lean forward and brush my lips against his cheek.

He doesn't jump the way I half expect him to. He's surprised, but the corners of his mouth lift just a bit, letting me know it wasn't a bad surprise. "Here," he says again, tapping the exit on the map. "We'll meet right here."

And then we split up.

CAPTURE

Suppressing my instinct to run is physically painful, as is restraining the worst-case-scenario thoughts that hit me with every step I take.

The hat is too big. It's not adjustable either, so it keeps dipping forward and covering half my face, which I realize might not be a bad thing. Still, it would have fit Malcolm better, and helped conceal his appearance, because we both need to walk out of here undetected.

There are several residents milling about, some who take the time to smile at me as I pass and others who give me blank stares as they shuffle along. Goose bumps rise on my skin, knowing that Malcolm and I are moving farther and farther apart.

Malcolm's right about this place being understaffed. Still, I check around each corner before entering a new hall, and if I see any employees, I slip inside a room and wait for them to pass. Not all the rooms are unoccupied, though, and I waste precious seconds with lies explaining my presence to the residents who ask who I am.

I enter the passcode wrong on the first try when I reach the door leading to the hall in front of the stairs. Fortunately, Malcolm had the foresight to memorize the codes for every floor, and he made me repeat the one I needed three times before I left. I take a deep breath and try again. This time, the red light turns green, and I use my key to open the door before picking up speed and nearly tripping as I rush down the steps. It's even harder to rein in the impulse to run once I'm on the ground floor, but I do it. I suck in a deep breath, and I stroll down the first hall.

Amble down the second.

And saunter up the third.

When I see the security guard standing by the exit, my muscles relax fractionally, because Malcolm was right again. This guy has a white-knuckled grip on his radio, and I can see a sheen of sweat on the wide expanse of his forehead even from yards away.

I don't charge him, though. Not yet.

I force my legs to bend, and I lower myself onto a bench as though I'm waiting for someone.

Well, I *am* waiting for someone, but my easy, nonthreatening movement and, more than likely, the facial-feature-and-hair-hiding hat cause the guard to skim right past me in his vigilant defense of the exterior door.

I wait another minute for Malcolm. Two minutes, three . . .

He likely also had to avoid a staff member or two by hiding out in rooms. And he's hurt, I remind myself. That fall outside my grandfather's room hadn't done his ribs any favors.

Another minute passes, I know this because there's a clock on the wall directly across from me and I've been tracing the second hand like my life will be over if I so much as blink. I'm staring so hard at it that I don't notice him until he slides onto the bench next to me.

"Ready to charge a security guard?"

The guard lost, and now we're outside.

And we're okay.

We made it.

I turn to smile at Malcolm. I know we still have to put some distance between us and Silver Living, but that seems easy by comparison.

I don't see either man until Malcolm and I are ripped away from each other. A pale, bony hand clamps over my mouth as an arm hooks tight around my waist and lifts my feet off the ground.

Malcolm is struck from behind, hard, and he goes down, but then another man, wearing black steel-toed boots, heaves him over his shoulder and starts walking toward a windowless van with the engine still running.

I scream, or try to, but the hand covering my mouth muffles the sound, so I bite down until the copper taste of blood fills my mouth.

I hit the pavement with teeth-rattling impact, but I manage to avoid slamming my head this time. Still, my legs are shaky, and I'm scrambling to try to get my feet under me.

All the while, I hear the man swearing. "Stupid little . . . Bit my hand . . ."

I scream when he grabs my ankle. I kick out and am rewarded with a grunt, but my attacker doesn't let go. I claw at the asphalt, desperate to find something to use as a weapon.

With a violent twist, he flips me onto my back, and the air punches out of my lungs as he lands a vicious kick to my ribs. I gasp, and my eyes stream with tears, blurring my vision.

He bends over me. "Little girls should not"—he kicks me again—"act"—another kick—"like"—I try to curl in on myself as he draws back for yet another kick—"fu—"

I drive my heel into his groin. He comes crashing down in a red-faced heap beside me, so close that only inches separate our faces. He has crystal-clear blue eyes, flooded with hate.

Pushing away, I whimper as I try to sit. I don't have time to wait for the pain to stop. I have to get up. I have to run. Now.

My body doesn't want to obey, and I can't straighten all the way when I stand, but I still move. Not remotely fast, but I move.

Malcolm. I see his unconscious body flung into the back

of the van, and the other man—the bounty hunter—turns and sees me. He casts one disgusted look at the man still writhing on the ground and starts after me.

I try to run. I swear I try. I know it's not enough. I don't look back, but I hear his footsteps growing closer, closer, and the sound stabs into me.

"No, no," I whisper, the words mingling with the sob I can't hold back.

And then there's bright-white pain splitting my skull.

TRAP

A sliver of light cuts my eyes as I pry them open, revealing a world that is upside down and swinging slowly from side to side.

The backs of two jean-covered thighs fill my vision, and my side throbs as we—me and the man whose shoulder I'm flung over—continue ascending a narrow staircase. I blink to better clear my vision, but the light is dim and my head screams at me to stop.

A few steps down a creaky hallway, I hear a door wrench open, and I'm lowered and dropped onto a hardwood floor. The impact is so sudden that I cry out.

"Wakey, wakey, little girl." It's Blue Eyes. He bends down, and I can feel his sour breath in my face. I try to turn away, but he grabs my chin in a crushing grip and forces me to face him. "I hope you don't tell the investigator anything when he gets here. Because then I'll be the one who gets to make you talk."

His fingers force my mouth to open. "First thing I'm gonna do is pull every one of these pretty teeth out. Two hours, maybe less, and you're mine."

"Move," another voice says, and I hear the difference in his steps as Blue Eyes backs away to make room. There's a subtle metal clang that tells me it's the bounty hunter. The light is so dim that all I see is his silhouette and the outline of a body over his shoulder.

Malcolm.

I don't know if I say his name out loud, but I whimper when he drops down beside me without so much as a twitch. I don't breathe when I press my fingers against his neck until I feel the steady beat of his pulse.

Unconscious. Not . . . anything else.

And then the door is shut, and a blackness surrounds me that's so complete I can't stop my hands from digging into Malcolm's chest.

In the impenetrable darkness, my other senses fire to life: the damp, musty wood from the floor or the walls, the slight bite of metal lingering on my fingers from the railing in the stairway at Silver Living, and the increasingly rapid breaths from Malcolm. He's practically shaking.

"Malcolm?"

Lurching from the floor, he flings himself at the door, pounding and rattling the knob in a panicked frenzy. The door is solid oak, and the hinges are on the outside—

I remember that much from before the light went out—so there's no way we can break it down. Even if we could, we'd just barrel right into the bounty hunter and Blue Eyes. My tongue instinctively runs over the teeth he promised to pull out, and I can't think of anything I want less than his hands on me again.

Malcolm has abandoned the door and is now ricocheting from one wall to the next, like a trapped animal, not caring what he crashes into or if he hurts himself. My hands find him easily in the small space, and I lock on to his shoulders.

"Stop. We need to think."

His movements halt, but his breathing remains frenetic. "I never used to be afraid of the dark. I feel like I'm back alone in my trunk. Tell me I'm not."

His muscles are flinching under my hands, and I squeeze. "You're not in the trunk. And you're not alone." We're so close that even though it's blacker than pitch, I'm aware of his head when he lowers it as if to look down, because I feel his too-fast breath on my upturned face.

"I can't see. Can you see? I can't—I can't—"

"Here." I slide my hands down his arms to his hands, shift us to what I'm approximating is the center of the room, and lift his arms with my own. "Feel the space?"

His fingers extend under mine, and for a second they intertwine before his greater reach surpasses mine and he's not encountering anything else. His breathing steadies some, but not all the way, so I shift his arms straight up, my hands on his forearms because of his extra height. "What do you feel?"

"Nothing," he says, in a full-body exhalation.

That's the moment I feel his awareness shift—from the claustrophobic space to the inch separating our bodies. He breathes in again, this time not to calm himself. I don't know how I know it's different, but I do. He lowers his arms a little until his hands are touching mine again, until a finger slides across my palm and I shiver and pull away.

"Are you okay now?"

"No," he says. "I'm pretty sure I'm going to freak the hell out again as soon as you move away." He very deliberately reaches for my hand again. "So don't, okay?"

There's a tremor in his voice that lets me know he's not just saying that as an excuse. The warmth from his hand seeps into mine, and my muscles begin to tense. I can't just stand there and hold his hand. There are too many things that I don't want to think about. Too many things that I can't think about. I swallow and hope he can't hear it. "I'm not going anywhere."

"Okay, that's not helping. I'm trying not to think about the fact that we're locked in a dark room barely bigger than your closet." His breath starts to speed back up, and I force his arms high again.

"See? Space. More than you remember. You can't even touch the ceiling. If you could reach," I say, "all you'd feel is—" I stop. "Wait, what did you say?"

I'm still touching him, so I feel it when he goes utterly still. The darkness takes on a new weight, and suddenly it's like it's pressing in on me, constricting.

"You told me before that you were in my house, in the hall outside my room, but that you refused go in. So how do you know what my closet looks like?"

SPY

Suddenly, as exhausted and scared and sore as I am, and as much I thought he was the reason I was staying strong, I pull away from him. "You lied."

He doesn't deny it, though I hear his breath catch the moment I stop touching him.

"I didn't technically lie. I—"

"Come on, stop." I'm too tired to cut him off with anything close to force. The words just fall out of my mouth as I rub my side from where Blue Eyes kicked me. "Are you working with *them*?" He doesn't need to see my head nod toward the direction of the door to know who I'm talking about. The darkness may be hiding my face and the tremble in my chin, but my voice gives me away.

"No, Katelyn. No." I feel the brush of his fingers as he reaches out for me, and I recoil. "You saw me, touched me. You know this isn't fake."

He means his injuries, but all I can think about is that I did touch him. I held his hand, held *him,* and, worse, I took comfort from that contact. I even kissed him.

And he was lying.

"You just never cared, did you?" That's the truth. I don't yell the words or spit them at him; I simply state the facts and let him do with them what he will.

"When I took this job, I didn't care about your mom or justice or anything," Malcolm says. "It was a challenge, that's all. I wanted to see if I could do it—find her when so many others failed. She wasn't real to me. It was like a game, one that I got paid to play."

Something slimy twists up from my stomach. He has no excuse, none. He was *playing* with my life, mine and Mom's, and we lost. It's little consolation that he lost too. In fact, it's no consolation at all. It's justice.

At least now I know.

He's still talking, though, which baffles me. Why would he think I want to hear a single thing more from him?

"Do you know how long it took me to find you after you uploaded that pic?"

Yeah, I know exactly, tired or not: two hours from post to pursuit. The consequences of that foolish decision blaze over my face before searing deep in my chest.

"About six minutes," he says.

The hot blood coursing through my cheeks chills.

"That's how long it took my program to flag you, trace you, and RAT your laptop."

"What? You did what?"

"I saw you through the camera when you opened your laptop and pretended to be doing your homework," he says. "You were smiling, happy, and I—it wasn't a game anymore. I was supposed to send the location to the investigator as soon as I found your mom, and then he would send whoever was closest to grab her. But the bounty hunter decided to cut out the competition as soon as he heard I'd been brought on, by setting up a camera in my house. He was at my door within ten minutes of your mom's face filling my computer screen, which is nine minutes and fifty-nine seconds longer than it would have taken me to send her location to the investigator." His voice shifts into something quieter, as though he's reliving the memory. "I was having doubts from the minute I found out that you existed. Not about your mom, not then, but about you and how I might be destroying your life. I refused to give him your address, and I held out as long as I could. It was only a couple of hours, but . . ."

Two hours. That's how long it took for Mom to get home and for us to run. If they'd gotten to us even five minutes sooner, we'd have never escaped in time.

"It's still my fault, but I wasn't depraved about you."

"What am I supposed to say?"

"Nothing," he says, raising a hand. "I just—I'm sorry. For everything."

I'm thinking about him getting beaten. I'm thinking about him living in a pitch-black trunk for three days. But I'm also

149

thinking of him watching me through my laptop, and searching for Mom without a care until he was forced to stare at me face to face. I'm thinking about Mom, wherever she is, separated from me because Malcolm did point the way.

And he's asking me to be better than him, to view his life alongside mine. Because he grew a conscience at the eleventh hour.

I don't know what to do with that. With any of it.

I look at the direction his voice came from. "I hate that you watched me. That you spied on me. You cannot understand what that feels like."

"Katelyn, I—"

"No," I say. It's a guttural whispered word. "If you'd told me back at the motel, it would have been just one more part of what you did to me, but you lied. You waited until I started to trust you, to care about what happened to you."

"I should have told you about watching you, okay? I was going to at the gas station before the cop came. Not because I thought you'd find out, but because I wanted you to know, even if you reacted just like this. I don't know how else to tell you I'm sorry. I don't even know what's true anymore." He's talking faster now, and I can hear the panic laced though his voice. He's moving a lot, twitching again, and I'm pretty sure his hands are still outstretched, searching for mine so that a simple touch can remind him he's not alone in the blackness.

"Katelyn?" He trying but failing to whisper. "Katelyn!"

"They're going to hear you," I say. My voice is watery, and I hate that.

I tell myself it's just to keep him quiet when I lift my arm and allow him to seize my hand with an audible sigh. His breathing has steadied when he starts talking again.

"I wasn't sure before, about your mom's guilt, but now, I honestly don't know. If Derek is your father, then everything the Abbotts said about the night he died is a lie."

All the thoughts that I've held at bay since finding my grandfather crash over me. My back is already resting against a wall, but I push harder against it, not caring that it causes pain to flare out from my bruised ribs. I tug my hand free from Malcolm's and wrap my arms around my chest.

I won't break in front of him. I won't. But my lungs fill and empty in rapid succession, and I know it's not sweat dripping down my cheeks. If Mom were here, I wouldn't be falling apart like this. I'd be raging, yelling, having the biggest, loudest knock-down, drag-out fight of our lives, worse than the time I found spyware she'd installed on my phone. Worse than the time I spotted her car outside my friend April Lancaster's house during my first-ever sleepover.

Every part of my life might be a lie. My name, my age, even my father. I double over at that last thought. When I think about my dad, I don't conjure up a beach-blond young man with a perfectly white smile and a sailboat bearing his name. I think of a man with perpetual coffee breath and a bit of paunch who carried me up to bed when I fell asleep watching TV.

All the lies. All the lies. Everything.

Malcolm may have doubts about Mom's guilt, but for the first time, I'm no longer sure of her innocence.

I don't push him away when he moves so that our shoulders are touching. The proximity to another person calms him instantly, whereas I feel like every part of me is fraying, splitting, disintegrating.

"We need to get out of here," he says.

I don't answer.

"Did you see anything when they brought us in?"

More silence from me.

"Katelyn? Come on. You can't shut down now."

But I can. I sink to the ground, and Malcolm has no choice but to follow me.

"No, no, no, no," he whispers. "You still want answers, right? You still want to know what happened. You've got the sonogram and this"—I flinch when his fingers brush my neck and he lifts my necklace from inside my shirt—"which prove that the 'infatuated teenager' who supposedly turned homicidal when she was rejected never existed. At the very least, there was a lot more involved with your mom than the Abbotts let on. He was planning to marry her."

There's something strange about the way Malcolm says that last part, something I would have pounced on even a few hours ago, but now I ignore it. "She lied about everything and now you believe her?" I say. "Or not even her. She's not the one standing here proclaiming her innocence. She left me, promised I'd be safe, and never came back. Maybe the truth is that she's running, even from me, because she *is* guilty."

"You don't believe that."

"I don't know what I believe." It hurts so much to say that, because it's true.

"No," Malcolm says. "I'm not *asking* you if you believe that. I'm telling you. Do you even know what you've done since she left? You outran a trained hunter. You basically took me hostage and extorted every dime I have to my name to get where you needed to go. You blackmailed me into sneaking you inside a surveilled building. Yeah, we got caught and locked up, but you wouldn't have done any of that if you thought for a moment your mom was a killer. And even though it's probably not the smartest thing I've ever done to bring this up again, I watched you two together before any of this started. I've never seen love like that. Not with me and my dad. Not even with me and my gran, because she's always still afraid that . . . well, that I'll do something like I did with this job. Your mom didn't have that with you. She lied about a lot of stuff, but not about loving you. And you don't need me to tell you that, do you?"

I think about Mom wriggling out of her Spanx as we laughed over her terrible first date, the one she'd gone on not because she wanted to, but because I'd asked her to try. I think about the fear in her face when we ran from our house, when she tended my injured head at the motel, when she had to leave me there. She'd been afraid for me, not for herself—not because her past had finally caught up with her, but because it had caught up with me.

I think about hiking instead of going to Disneyland, about the survival "games" she taught me, like locating possible exits in every building we entered instead of playing Candy Land or Guess Who? like other kids. I think of the miles we ran together every morning—even when it was raining, even when I didn't want to.

Because she knew that one day I might have to run, and hide, and escape.

"Tomorrow's my birthday," I say. "Tomorrow, I'm turning eighteen, not seventeen. Tomorrow, I'll be a legal adult." My heart pounds harder with every word. "She told me that when the time was right, she would be the one to pay for her mistake, not me. I think I know what she meant. Tomorrow's the day her actions, past, present, or future, stop blowing back on me."

Malcolm swears, and not quietly.

"Is she turning herself in?" I ask.

"I obviously don't know her like you do, but I don't think so."

"Because you don't think she did it?"

"Do you?"

I hesitate. "I know she loves me. That's enough for now.

And I know I've got to find her before she does something that will take her away from me for the rest of her life."

Malcolm squeezes my hand and pulls us both to our feet. "If you can use all the stuff your mom taught you to get us out of here, I swear I can find her. But, you know, keep talking, okay? I'm trying to keep it cool here, but it's like I can feel the walls and ceiling closing in." I know he's not faking the tremor that shudders through him.

"The man who brought me here said an investigator is coming to question me. How long do you think we have?"

He doesn't answer, and my pulse skips.

"Malcolm, we can't be here when he gets here."

"Then how do we get out?"

BREAKOUT

I close my eyes even though I can see nothing with them open. I envision the room in the brief time I saw it before the door was shut. There was a futon and a small wooden chair with spindle legs. No windows. I tilt my head back, opening my eyes to no avail, trying to remember if there was anything beyond the bulb hanging above. I find the switch right away, but flipping it does nothing. I turn away from Malcolm and have to ignore the sound of protest he makes when I start shuffling forward. When my shins bang into the side of the futon, I scramble on top, standing with my free hand stretched to the ceiling while the other is being squeezed way too tightly by Malcolm.

"Katelyn? What are you doing?"

I pause my exploration of the ceiling and reach blindly in front of me, stepping down to the floor and inching forward until the fingertips of my free hand brush against Malcolm's head. I glide them down to his shoulders, bending forward until my mouth accidentally bumps his ear.

"Hey, hey!" he says, leaning back and standing. "That's a little more distraction than I need, but—"

I pull his head back to my mouth, rising on my toes and not caring when my lips graze his ear again. Dropping my voice to a barely audible volume, I say, "I'm trying to talk to you without being overheard." Just because we can't hear anyone outside the door doesn't mean they aren't there, especially after the way our voices rose when we forgot ourselves. "I'm checking the ceiling for an access hatch to the attic. I can't remember if I saw one or not. Do you?"

Malcolm is shifting under my hands with every word, and it's only when he turns his head to whisper in my own ear that I understand why. We're practically cheek to cheek. His breath is warm, and it stirs the tiny hairs along my neck, making me shiver just as he had. "I didn't come to until they shut the door."

"It'll be faster if we both search. Will you be okay if I let go of you?"

"Are you going to think less of me if I say no?"

"Probably," I say with a slight smile he can't see. The fact that he can joke about it means he'll keep it together.

Without further need for communication, he steps up on the chair and I return to the futon. The quiet scuffing I hear is him moving the chair around.

"Katelyn."

Just my name. I follow his voice, and when I reach the chair, he steps down for me to take his place. The ceiling is plaster, and rough under my fingertips, so I know the second I encounter the smooth rounded trim that surrounds a scuttle hole. Malcolm's hand is resting on the outside of my leg just above the knee for balance, since the chair, like everything else in the room, is on its last legs. I reach down and squeeze his hand. Yes, this is what I was hoping for. The panel isn't big, maybe two feet square, but compared to the jagged window opening I squeezed through at the motel, it'll be cake.

I step back to the floor and, still holding Malcolm's hand, pull him as far away from the door as possible—six feet, maybe. I don't get quite as close to him when I whisper this time. "I don't remember seeing a pull-down in the hallway, so this must be the only access to the attic. It's been completely painted over; we'll have to score the edges to open it. Maybe that's a sign they forgot it's in here."

Malcolm's cheek brushes against mine. "And maybe not."

We're still close enough that he can feel me nod. "It's our best option." Malcolm doesn't need to see me to understand the urgency behind that statement. Yes, I'm terrified of Blue Eyes, but there's no physical pain worse than not finding my mom.

"But we can get out through there?" he says.

"It's the only way out of this room I can see." Which doesn't answer his question. I have no idea what we'll find in the attic by way of an exit, but it has to be more than we have now. "We need something sharp to loosen the panel from the paint." I look up again, imagining the lightbulb overhead. "I could break the bulb, but it might be too delicate." And it might cut my hands to shreds in the dark.

Malcolm turns away from me, and I hear him shuffling around the room. There's not much to search. The whole space *is* about the size of my closet. The shuffling grows louder, and the pounding of my heartbeat grows with it. I don't want our jailers hearing noises they can't account for.

"Don't worry," I say in my normal volume. "I'll explain everything to the investigator when he gets here. We're safe for now. We just have to wait."

Malcolm falls silent, and I wonder if he doesn't realize I was talking for the dual benefit of Blue Eyes and the bounty hunter and to cover his rustling, but then he replies just as clearly.

"You're right." He stands, and his hand touches my arm, following it up to my shoulder. Leaning in, he whispers, "I need your earring."

The studs are tiny emeralds that Mom got me for my last birthday, sixteenth or seventeenth, whichever one it actually turns out to have been. When I find her, Mom and I will have the mother of all fights—after I finish hugging her for three days straight. I never take the earrings out. When I cut and colored my hair that morning, shedding my former skin, I hadn't even considered removing them. But I do it now without hesitation, handing over the small but precious piece of jewelry.

We keep talking about nothing after that, our voices loud and clear, and moments later Malcolm presses not just my earring back into my hand, but also a short screw that he must have taken from the futon frame.

"Will that work?" he says softly.

"Only one way to find out."

We intersperse our random conversation with whispers detailing our progress as I take over securing our escape route. I slide the edge of the screw around the inner edge of the panel. The paint is thick, and due to the damp air, not as yielding as I'd like. I have the palm of my left hand pressed flat against the panel, pushing with steady, sustained force and trying to discern even the slightest give.

Our height difference isn't so great that my standing on the chair puts Malcolm and me at eye level, but it's small enough that bending down a little allows me to reach him without having to pause in my task.

"Two sides are lifting," I say in his ear, excitement joining the words together. Malcolm's hand on my shoulder keeps me from straightening.

"You don't have to forgive me," he says. "For any of this. Me saying I'm sorry doesn't mean I expect that from you." He drops his hand, but I don't move away. "I just need you to know that, whatever happens. And thank you for saving my life at the motel. I don't think I told you that."

My breath catches. We've been speaking in hushed voices,

whispers so soft that we have to press into each other to make them out. Right now, I'm leaning into him and he's holding my head to his. It's an embrace, and there's no escaping the feel of his heartbeat thudding against mine.

"Why didn't you just tell him what he wanted to know?" I say. "He wouldn't have kept you in the trunk for all those days."

"I don't know." Something about the cadence of Malcolm's answer implies a shrug, but I don't let it go.

"I think you do," I say, testing the words on my tongue and finding I believe them. It's one thing to hesitate about turning over me and Mom, not knowing for sure what his actions would ultimately cost him. It's another to be tied up in the dark for days on end. "You gave us more time than you had to. Way more," I say with assurance.

I can tell he's looking toward me—knowing that he's free because of me, just like I know I got away because of him. He saved me before he even knew me.

I let out a shaky breath. For the first time since this nightmare started, I'm not tensed and ready to strike or bolt at the slightest provocation. I'm not sitting next to Malcolm with a weapon in my hand or smothered by my own fear of what lies ahead.

"I forgive you."

He goes statue-still; even his heart seems to pause as my words sink in. "Yeah?"

"But don't lie to me again."

"No, never. I've seen you with a blade."

Somehow, I know we're both smiling.

"Then let's get out of here."

Malcolm talks in a normal voice about his goldfish back at home, Stan and Ollie, while I attack the remaining two sides of the stuck panel. He won them two years ago at a carnival for a girl who tried to throw them away at the end of the night, which consequently didn't inspire him to ask for a second date.

I tell him about the café where I work and my best friends, Regina and Carmel. I grow a little morose thinking about them. By now, Regina will have convinced herself that she did something to warrant my complete vanishing act and Carmel, who's all too familiar with my mom's antics, probably thinks I'm in the middle of another impromptu move. She'll be making herself sick with worry until I call and tell her I'm okay. And Aiden . . . he predicted I'd bail on him, so if anything, he's blaming himself for not knowing better than to get involved with me. Maybe he's even eyeing someone new by now. That's what I should hope he's doing. The alternative is that he realized something bad happened and he's concerned about me. Or worse, he's gone to the authorities.

I can't deal with thinking about the people I care about right now, so I redouble my efforts with the panel. A minute later I stop. "Malcolm? I'm tired. Are you tired? I think we should try and get some sleep." I might have injected too much force into the word *sleep*, but the entire panel just lifted free from the last edge. I slide it to the side and rise on my toes so that the top of my head breaches the opening.

The attic, more of a crawl space really, runs the full length of the house, and under the canted roof it's crowded with boxes and various junk. Based on the thick layer of dust blanketing everything and the assorted mouse corpses on the floor, no one's been up here in a long time. Skimming past the rot and ruin, I see at last what allowed me to see any of it: a window.

The dim moonlight bleeding into the attic like a gloomy fog is barely better than the blackness below, but remembering Malcolm's claustrophobia, I tug his hand and make room for him on the chair so he can see it: light, however weak, and more space.

Crowded together, I whisper, "Can you get up?"

He doesn't answer. One second, he's beside me, and the next, his elbows are braced on either side of the opening, snowing dust down on both of us. He pulls himself up and through without a sound and turns back to lock arms with me.

"Wait." I step down and move the chair as close to the wall as possible while still letting me reach Malcolm. When our captors open that door—hopefully, a long time from now and not because we inadvertently make noise escaping—then every minute of confusion will count.

My cardio may be killer, but my upper-body strength is so pathetic that I find room on top of everything else to be embarrassed by how little I help Malcolm haul me up.

"Okay?" I ask when he clutches at his side. I can't tell if it's the poor light making him look so pale or the pain I know he just endured. He nods, waving me on.

My pace is glacial since I don't know which floorboards will creak—or worse, considering the condition of the wood. I slide one foot ahead of the other, ears alert, and wince as it becomes impossible to avoid the heavy curtains of spiderwebs hanging thick from every surface. I suppress a squeak as the first one tangles in my hair and still more stick to my arms. Something squishes under my foot, and I close my eyes to ignore the instinct to look down. I know it's a mouse. I know it. One not long dead, by the smell of it. I have to stop at one point to carefully and quietly migrate a stack of moldy boxes from my path. Malcolm moves the higher ones.

And then we see it clearly: our so-called escape. And I know without a doubt we're both thinking the same four-letter word.

LEAP

"Shit." Malcolm says it out loud.

I'm still staring, so I don't think to caution him about his volume. It is a window, but it's gotta be prison-regulation, because there is no way that it can be crawled out of.

"I can fit," I say anyway, and Malcolm's eyes immediately drop to my hips.

"Not all of you."

I spare a flicker of energy to be offended.

He lifts his hands. "I'm not complaining about the visual, just pointing out the size discrepancy between that child-size window and us."

"Both of us can fit."

He opens his mouth to protest again, then shuts it. "Okay. How?"

"However we have to."

There it is. We can fit out this window the size of a license plate because there is no alternative. We can't go back to our cell and wait for our jailers, or the investigator who hired them; this is the only opening. If we have to find a working chain saw in one of these boxes and go roaring through, then that's what we'll do.

Luckily, like everything else in the attic, the window is rotting. We're able to pry the frame free with just our fingers and gain an inch or two on all sides. A desperate prisoner emaciated to near-skeletal condition could make it out now, but that still excludes Malcolm, me, and my hips.

There isn't any drywall or insulation in the attic, so once we get rid of the wood we're left with brick and mortar, which has fared much more favorably over the years. I could work my fingers to the bone—and likely would—trying to dislodge only one brick, let alone the dozen we'd need, and we'd still be trapped inside.

Defeat pulls at me, trying to force me to the ground. Malcolm is just standing there—half bent over because of the low ceiling—waiting for me to figure a way out.

Meanwhile, Mom is maybe preparing to turn herself in over a death that's not as clear-cut as the authorities believe.

I reach a hand outside and let the moonlight envelop it. Rain has started spitting, and more will come. The gutters along the streets will flood, and roofs will leak. And we'll be here banging our heads against a brick wall. The window might as well have bars.

That last thought hits me like a slap in the face. If Malcolm had said it, I would have hit him. Probably more than once. Giving up is not an option. Regrouping is. Reassessing is. Finding a way when there isn't one.

I pull my arm back inside. At least the spiderwebs have been washed away. The ones in my hair are more stubborn, but they relent eventually. When they're off me at last, I cast new eyes around the attic. "Somewhere, there is a way out," I say. "We haven't looked hard enough yet." I don't say it may be in the form of an ancient shotgun that we use to blow off the door to the room below and hold our captors at gunpoint until they let us go, but I allow for the possibility.

We are getting out of this house.

Malcolm is the one who finds it, or hears it. Birds tweeting. In a corner eave of the roof, where brick meets wood and shingle, a robin is nesting.

"She burrowed in," he says. "Why can't we burrow out?"

We both see the waterlogged boxes, a stack right by the scuttle hole that neither of us had looked at in our eagerness to reach the window. The roof has leaked in this spot, not a lot, and probably just recently, but once again our faces are tilted up and our hands are pulling down. The storm has picked up, adding in rolls of thunder and sharp cracks of lightning. We break through sodden plywood and roofing, synchronizing each impact with the thunder as best we can, balancing our desire for urgency with our need to remain unheard.

Time exists only in the strikes and rumbles of the storm, but as more rain beats down on us through our ever-widening hole, the faster we work. We stop the second we both agree my hips and his shoulders will fit. Nothing tears at my flesh as Malcolm lifts me through the hole, and I'm not being pursued, making it infinitely better than the last tiny opening I had to force myself through.

I emerge onto the rooftop into a mass of oak leaves and branches that dump chilled water down my collar, soaking me instantly, but I press them back and move so Malcolm can pull himself up. Once he gets his shoulders through, the rest of him comes out easily enough. We grin at each other as rain pelts us and lightning crashes near enough for the scent of ozone to fill the air.

I skirt out from under the dense canopy, searching for a branch thick enough for us to climb down. The one I find is not within arm's distance of the roof, no matter how close I stand to the edge. But it is, I think, within jumping distance. If I were on the ground, I'd know I could make it. Without a running start, in the pouring rain and cloudy night, I'm less confident.

Before I can talk myself out of it, I leap.

The bark is thick and scratchy against my palms as I catch hold of the branch, with my feet hanging below. My grip feels sure, so I swing myself so that the tips of my shoes reach a larger branch below. Inhaling rapidly a few times, I rock my body forward at the same time that I release my hands. After a split second of blind terror, my upper body overtakes my lower and I wrap my arms tightly around the gnarled trunk of the tree.

Turning, I find Malcolm watching me with raised eyebrows from the edge of the roof, one arm still bracing his ribs. My body definitely did not enjoy my Tarzan act, so I can only imagine what his will do. He's blinking furiously, maybe because of the rain streaming into his eyes, maybe because he can see exactly how high up we are and that there's nothing below to break his fall beyond a minuscule woodpile.

Despite how slippery and precarious my position feels, I give up one handhold and extend an arm, beckoning. I don't dare risk calling out to him.

I venture a step closer to the house. He has to jump. He's taller than me, with demonstrably more upper-body strength, but he's also injured, and we've had to rely on his much-abused ribs too much already.

The sight is terrifying. He hits the first branch with an impact that reverberates through the trunk, and grimacing, he drops a hand. Dangling from one arm, he pumps his legs and lets go the second they're over the branch I'm on. We collide into each other, me grabbing him, him pinning us both to the trunk.

My breath comes out in a whoosh, and I can feel his heart pounding beneath his rib cage. Mine is pounding too.

"Nice catch," he says before hugging me, without any pretense of holding us to the tree. My arms are already around him, but I shift them and hug him back in the rain.

Malcolm insists on climbing down the tree first. "In case I fall, I won't take you out with me."

I doubt that would happen, after seeing his one-armed catch, but I take his point and let him pick out the strongest branches before following. We look back at the house repeatedly during our relatively speedy descent, but I'm only seconds behind him when he hits the ground.

Hand in hand, we run.

DITCH

Our post-prison-break swim through the suburbs is wet and cold. And I'm legitimately worried by some of the groans Malcolm is making with increasing regularity.

"Okay?" I call out over the heavy rain.

He nods, and we keep moving. He's not, though. He's been listing more and more to his left, but when I move around him to offer my shoulder, he waves me off almost angrily.

I don't feel too hot either.

My side hurts, but I do my best to ignore the throb. It's my head that claims all my attention. Every jarring footstep sends a corresponding jolt through my temples. I prod the base of my skull as we run and wince at the swelling goose egg. Glancing over at Malcolm, I don't need to search for the spot where he was hit. It looks like he has a golf ball stitched onto the side of his head.

His toe catches on a square of sidewalk that a nearby oak

lifted with its roots, and I have to catch him before he goes down.

"Stop. Malcolm, we have to stop." I pull him under the shelter of the tree's dense branches, and we huddle together, shivering for more reasons than the temperature. My body tells me we've run a half marathon. My head tells me we've gone maybe a mile or two.

Not far enough. Not nearly far enough.

We're still in suburbia. Friendly scarecrows are staked in the freshly mown lawns of red brick middle-class homes. Hastily abandoned bikes line both sides of the street. Artfully carved pumpkins decorate every porch. The grass is still green even as the oak trees that guard the neighborhood have all turned golden, crimson, and rust.

But there's nowhere to go. Not even a conveniently unlocked garage.

I've been looking.

"Okay, I did my part," I say—pant, really. "Where's my mom?"

Malcolm laughs at my bad joke. "Get me a computer."

"Sure," I say. "Anything else?" He doesn't laugh this time. "How much farther can you walk?"

"Not far." The weariness in his voice tells me he's overestimating even that. "It's like fire, every step, but sharp." His hand drifts to the hem of his shirt but then moves away, as though he doesn't want to see the skin underneath. Or he already knows how bad it is.

"Malcolm," I say softly, my gaze forcibly lifting from his side to his face. "Maybe you should—"

But he's shaking his head, cutting off my offer before I can even make it. "I promised we'd find your mom. I owe you that much. I'll be all right till then."

My stomach clenches. If he hadn't added those last two words, I'd have let myself believe him. But every second I force him to run or jump off roofs, or even stand, puts him at more risk. For all I know, his cracked ribs have fully broken—that is, if they weren't broken before. Maybe the hairline fractures have split wide and cut his insides and he's bleeding internally. I blanch at the thought.

Turning my head, I look for the closest house with a car in its driveway and lights on inside and head straight toward it. He's not fine. But he will be.

"What are you . . . Where are you going?"

"To get you help. You need to go to the hospital, Malcolm. We both know that."

"Wait." He takes a lurching step after me. "Will you wait!" The sudden strength in his voice stops me, and he straightens more than I thought he could. "You still need me."

"Not if you're hurt. Not if helping me hurts you more." The rain is so torrential now that my mouth fills with water every time I open it to speak. "And you don't owe me anything anymore. I'm not holding a weapon or forcing you. You don't even know me." I try to laugh. "I can't help you with the money, but I won't say anything about you to anyone, okay? You can go. No hard feelings. I can figure the rest out on my own. I don't know how, but I will."

Malcolm's eyes narrow, his brows drawing closer together. "Are you done?"

I frown. "If you're ready to let me get you to a hospital I am."

He licks his lips. His glare intensifies.

"Is that your guy way of saying yes without having to say so?"

"You are a piece of work. You know that?"

For a moment, his words hurt more than all the aches and throbs in my body combined. I don't understand why he's so angry. I'm giving him exactly what he wanted back at the motel. This is his out. "Why are you acting like I'm the bad guy all of a sudden?" I say. "I'm trying to do the right thing!"

"No, you're not," he says. "You're trying to do the thing you think makes you look strong. It doesn't. I'm not about to keel over here, okay? My ribs hurt like a mother, and I'm tired, I'm cold, I'm hungry. I'm all the things you are, so stop trying to ditch me when we both know you don't have any idea where to go next."

"Oh, and you do?"

"Yeah, actually. I do."

My eyes narrow. I don't know him well enough to tell if he's bluffing. But why would he?

"This is not me lying to you," he says, brows smoothing as his voice adopts a less hostile tone. "This is me telling you as soon as we didn't have to focus all our attention on getting out of that place, okay?"

I'm soaked through and shivering again, but it's his words that set my teeth chattering. I can't take another bomb right now. I just can't.

"Never looked into Derek before. I didn't think he mattered. Honestly, the first news story about him that I even watched was that one with you at the motel. But after the sonogram, I had this nagging thought in my mind, like I was forgetting something, overlooking it, you know, because it wasn't important before."

"Malcolm." I need him to just say it.

"When we split up at Silver Living, I was late meeting you because I had to check, make sure I was wrong. I wasn't." His lungs visibly inflate and deflate, but the only sign of discomfort is a small twitch in his cheek. "The night Derek died, it wasn't just him and his parents having dinner when your mom showed up. His wife was there too. His very pregnant wife."

RIDE

"You might have a half sister," Malcolm says.

A sister. A sister. I repeat the words in my head over and over again. We're standing in the middle of someone's lawn, and I might have a sister.

I lift my gaze to his. I don't know how he can tell that there's anything more than rain on my face, but he moves toward me, and slowly, like he knows I might not welcome the gesture but he's offering it anyway, Malcolm hugs me.

I sink into him, my arms coming up to clutch his shoulders, and I notch my head beneath his chin.

A sister.

And Mom knew. She was there. She would have seen Derek's wife that night at the Abbott estate, even if she somehow didn't know before. I want to believe she didn't know Derek was married, but I can't make things true just by wanting them to be. Mom might have entered willingly into an affair with a married man who had a pregnant wife. I can't imagine her doing something like that now, but nearly twenty years ago? If she did that . . .

I jerk away from Malcolm and the comforting warmth of his body, of him. Whatever else she did, whatever lies she felt she had to tell, whatever things she kept from me, she isn't now, then, or ever capable of killing anyone.

That is the one truth I don't have to wish into existence.

Malcolm looks at me so long I think he's going to start chipping away at the fragile footing I've found.

"Laura," Malcolm says while I make a poor attempt at trying to compose myself. "That's Derek's widow. She lives here in Pennsylvania. I didn't have a lot of time, but as far as I could tell, she never gave a single interview—TV, newspaper—nothing. I had to dig to find a current address, because the woman doesn't want to be found almost as much as your mom."

"But you did find it?"

Malcolm gives me a "Come on" look, like the question is almost an insult.

"Then we've got to get to her," I say. "If she was there that night, then she knows everything. Maybe that's why she shunned the press. Maybe the Abbotts paid her off, or maybe . . ." Different scenarios tumble in my brain, and several spill from my lips before Malcolm quiets me when his fingers reach for mine.

"I looked for her because . . . I honestly I don't know why.

Maybe so you could know. But, Katelyn . . ." His hand slips higher to fully envelop mine. He squeezes, once. "You can't go see her. You get that, right? Your mom is wanted for killing her husband. I'm not saying your mom did it," he adds as my eyes flare. "Just that she's been the primary—the only—suspect for almost two decades."

I tug my hand free. "I know that." I say it so quietly that the sound barely travels over the pouring rain.

"She doesn't even know you exist. I mean no one did or your mom would have been a lot easier to find, but you're still . . ." He trails off. "Your grandfather, the sonogram, the ring? It all fits. I believe you are Derek's daughter, and if you are, then you're proof that Laura's husband cheated on her. The second you tell her that . . . it's not going to be good."

"Then I won't tell her unless I have to." My arms wrap around my midsection at the gut-twisting reminder of my mom's lies. "I don't know what I'll tell her," I add, forestalling the question I see in Malcolm's eyes. "I'll come up with something, but I still have to go."

She might react violently if I tell her who I am—who I might be—or even call the police. She might break down on her porch in a sobbing mess, and my first meeting with the girl who could be my sister might be over the broken mess of her mother.

Grace. That's her name, Malcolm tells me. The pull to meet her is just as strong as the one wanting to hear Laura's side. Possibly even stronger.

Maybe Malcolm knows me better than I accused him of earlier, because no other protests leave his lips. Instead, he says, "Mrs. Laura Boyer lives with her new family, including Grace—though I couldn't even find a picture of her—in a house not far from the Abbotts', in Elkins Park. I don't know how long we were unconscious, but it can't have been that long." Malcolm glances around. "I mean, this looks like the same area Silver Living is in, maybe even still Cheltenham. Which means we're probably only twenty or thirty minutes away."

I give him a smile. It's a little shaky, but he returns it.

"Guess it's your turn again," he says. "How are we getting there? And just so you know, I'm not hiding any more cash in my other shoe."

I take a deep breath, letting my cheeks puff out when I release it, then turn on my heel. Mom did this, which means I can too. Taking Malcolm's hand, I lead us straight to the front door of the house I was intent on approaching earlier.

"Wait, wait. I thought—"

"Don't say a word," I tell him as I ring the bell.

A petite sandy-haired woman with glasses perched low on her nose and a sudoku book folded up under one arm answers the door. "Yes? Can I help— Oh my! Oh my goodness," she says, taking in our beaten drowned-rat appearance.

"I'm so sorry to bother you, but my boyfriend and I were in

a car accident, and both our phones were broken. We've been walking for"—I turn to Malcolm—"I don't know how long. Miles maybe?" He starts to open his mouth, but I turn back to her. "Would it be too much trouble if we came in so I could call my mom? We were driving down from college to surprise my little brother for his birthday, and I'm sure my mom is worried sick by now." I add a well-timed sneeze just to cinch the performance, and suddenly the woman—Mrs. Goodwin, she tells us—is clucking her tongue and ushering us inside to warm up by the fire.

Once we've assured her that our injuries are only superficial, she brings us towels to dry off and even offers us some of her kids' old clothes to wear while she tosses ours in the dryer. (Michael, Anne-Marie, and Kristen—all grown and with families of their own.)

After handing her our wet clothes, Malcolm and I meet in the Jack and Jill bathroom adjoining the separate bedrooms she showed us upstairs.

"Nice lady," he says.

I agree, already dreaming about the hot tea and food she promised us.

"Can you . . . ?" He gestures at his wet shirt as his mouth tightens. He doesn't like being so reliant on my help, and I don't like feeling responsible for him needing it, as least partially.

Instead of lifting his shirt, though, I bend down and open the cabinet under the sink, heart lifting when I find a well-stocked first-aid kit. We'll be able to tape Malcolm's ribs this time. That'll have to help.

I turn us around so our backs are to the mirror before inching his shirt up. I don't trust my face to remain impassive if he looks worse than before.

I wince as his torso is revealed.

Worse. Much worse. My raging appetite vanishes.

"Nothing's sticking out." There's something about the way Malcolm says it that makes me think he's surprised.

I worry my lip until he grabs the tape and slaps it in my hand. "Forget it. *We* are doing this. Now am I taping myself or not?"

I don't really know how to tape ribs, but I do my best, and Malcolm takes a testing breath when I'm done and says it feels a little better. But then, we've already raided the medicine cabinet and helped ourselves to some leftover painkillers.

"So what now?" Malcolm says after we're both dressed. "You know you can't call anyone you're close to. By now, they're being watched. Their phones might even be tapped."

I nod, thinking about Aiden. And Carmel and Regina and everyone else from the café where I work. *Worked*, I mentally correct myself. I've missed enough shifts by now that I've definitely been fired, though our neighbor Mr. Guillory probably still has no idea that Mom and I are the reason his car ended up in that Walgreens parking lot. More names and faces push themselves forward in my mind, and each one takes a swipe at my heart.

I have people that I miss, a life that I miss.

And I can't go back to any of them.

"I've got a plan," I say, hoping Malcolm doesn't notice that my voice has gone tight.

He doesn't. He's too busy fiddling with the collar on the pistachio-green polo shirt Mrs. Goodwin gave him. "What kind of grown man lets his mom still write his name on his tag?"

"No way," I say, glad for the distraction.

Malcolm turns around and squats a little so I can confirm that, yep, MICHAEL is written there in dark-blue Sharpie. I smother a laugh.

"Just be glad she didn't have three daughters." I didn't spot any names in the tags of the clothes she gave me—jeans and a chunky cable-knit sweater in ballet pink—but everything is a bit snug.

"Okay up there?" Mrs. Goodwin calls from the stairs.

Darting back to my room, I tell her we'll be right there.

Tea is steaming invitingly from two matching floral mugs when we get downstairs, alongside two heaping bowls of chili. My mouth instantly floods with saliva, and it's all I can do not to fall on the food like . . . like someone who hasn't eaten anything except a protein bar in the past three days.

"Mrs. Goodwin, that smells delicious."

She blushes. "It was my husband's favorite, God rest his soul. I gave you a lot since you both looked hungry. Phone's right there on the counter."

I take a step toward the phone, only to stop in the act of lifting the receiver to my ear, making sure Mrs. Goodwin sees me hesitate and bite my lip. "I can't believe I'm this stupid," I say. "My mom just got a new number. It was in my phone, but I don't have it memorized." I turn my worried gaze to Malcolm. "Do you know anyone's number?"

His eyes darting to Mrs. Goodwin before returning to me, Malcolm says between bites, "No?" There's a hint of a question in his voice, but Mrs. Goodwin doesn't seem to pick up on it.

Abandoning the phone, I drop forlornly into the chair beside him and glance at our host. "I bet Michael, Anne-Marie, and Kristen all know their friends' and families' numbers by heart."

"Ha" is Mrs. Goodwin's answer. "Michael loses his phone constantly. He wouldn't remember his own name if I didn't write it in his clothes. Kristen and Anne-Marie are little better." From across the table, she reaches out to pat my hand. "Is your parents' house far? I'd be happy to drop you off after you eat and warm up."

Malcolm seizes my knee under the table and I grin.

"That would be wonderful, Mrs. Goodwin. The address is . . ."

AMBUSH

Mrs. Goodwin leans across the front seat to hug me when we pull up in front of Laura's house. "Now you promise to call me after you get settled and celebrate your brother's birthday."

"I promise." She smells like the cinnamon she sprinkled in our tea, and I let myself breathe in the comforting scent. "And we'll get these clothes back to you too."

"Keep them. I've been meaning to donate them anyway. But come by and have tea with me again sometime." She glances to the backseat. "You too, Malcolm," she adds.

I tell her we're going to let ourselves in through the back door, to make sure she won't idle out front waiting to see us safely inside. Huddled together under the umbrella Mrs. Goodwin forced into our hands before she let us out of the car, we dart around the side of the house and watch her drive off.

Malcolm's squeezes an arm around my waist. "Still want to do this?"

184

No, I want to stare after the kind woman who gave me a sweater and fed me chili. I don't want to think about the woman whose life I'm about to destroy the second I ring her doorbell. But I nod.

There's no darting this time as we return to the front of the house and make our way up the brick walkway. The house is a three-story colonial, with white siding, crisp black shutters, and a trio of dormer windows extending from the pitched roof. The lawn is impeccably landscaped, with seasonal purple daisies, pink chrysanthemums, and golden false sunflowers on either side of the columned porch. It's a beautiful, lovingly kept home, though nowhere near as large or lavish as what I remember from the video of the Abbott estate, the home she likely would have one day lived in if Derek hadn't died.

Is she bitter about the loss of circumstances as well as the loss of her husband?

The front door is glossy black, and I don't want to lift my hand to knock on it.

But my sister could be inside.

Or her mother.

Or no one.

"You want me to . . . ?" Malcolm gestures at the door.

My headshake is tight and slight. I have to be strong now.

I knock.

She's wearing a cardigan sweater when she opens the door, and it's the same soft shade of pink as I'm wearing. Her hair is long and dark blond, with subtle honey highlights, and somehow it's not frizzy, despite the rain. Her makeup is equally understated, and there isn't a hint of a wrinkle in her lightly tanned forehead.

She's not frozen, though. Her features undergo a remarkable transformation after her cautiously polite greeting. One moment, she's looking at me with an untroubled expression lifting her delicately arched brows, and the next she's recoiling as all the blood drains from her face.

Her mouth opens.

"Mom!" A girl calls from upstairs. "I can't find my phone charger." Her voice is competing with the rain, so it's a little muffled, but I hear it and, without even thinking, I take a step forward.

"No!" The woman—Laura—stops me with a guttural whisper as her hand shoots out to clutch the doorframe and bar my entry. Then, in a voice that is all sweetness and ease, one that is at complete odds with the fierce expression on her face, she calls back, "I put it in your nightstand."

Malcolm, Laura, and I are as still as statues as we wait. Moments later, we hear, "Found it!"

Laura scans my face, a more thorough examination than the initial one. Nothing changes in her features, nothing, but I see the skin around her knuckles turn whiter where her hand is still wrapped around the door.

"You knew," I say, my voice an accusation and a statement all in one. It's so obvious now. I didn't have time to process the implications of her reaction when she first answered the door. But from the moment the girl upstairs spoke, the girl who has to be my sister, I couldn't think of anything else.

Laura recognizes me, and my skin itches like swarms of insects are skittering their tiny legs all over me.

"How do—"

She puts a hand up, and her nostrils flair in warning at the volume of my voice. I wasn't shouting, but I wasn't whispering either. It takes her only a second of stillness to make a decision, and then she snaps into motion.

"Inside," she says, forcing her arm down as she steps back, making room for Malcolm and me.

Malcolm's hand is warm and solid on my back, and I have no idea when he put it there, but I'm grateful for the encouragement to take that first step into the house of my father's widow.

NEGOTIATE

I don't notice a single thing about the house Laura leads us through, or the room she shuts us in. All the questions I need to ask, all the explanations I need, get tangled up together, and nothing comes out, not even after she closes the door and turns to face me again.

Laura has gotten over her shock. She stares at me less like the ugliest part of her past has been exhumed and crawled its way onto her porch, and more like she's resolved to contain and remove the nightmare as soon as possible.

"What do you want?" She doesn't ask who I am, doesn't waste time asking why I'm here. She gets right to the point, so I do exactly the same thing.

I lift my chin. "How do you know who I—"

I cut myself off because I already know the answer. There's only one other person alive who could have told her that Derek Abbott was my father. "When did my mother tell you about me?"

There it is again: the nostril flare. That subtle betrayal to the otherwise perfectly composed face. I think she's considering not telling me, but then we all hear footsteps from the floor above us. Grace clearly doesn't know about me, and if the performance at the front door is any indication, Laura is adamant that she never find out. Another nostril flare, and she starts talking.

"She didn't tell me. I saw the way she was holding her stomach that night. Like recognized like."

My heart freezes still when I ask my next question. "Did she kill him?"

Her eye twitches. "Yes."

"You're lying," I say, my voice breaking as I lunge forward.

Malcolm catches my arm to hold me back. Laura doesn't move.

"No," I say, shaking Malcolm off. "You knew who I was the second you saw me. I could have been a boy, or she could have miscarried. You knew who *I* was. *Me.*" I stab a finger into my chest, right over the ring hidden beneath my sweater. "What's my name?"

Another eye twitch. "I don't know."

I lock my jaw. "What's my name?"

"I told you, I don't—"

"Grace!" I call out. Not overly loud, but a warning. I take in a deeper breath. "Gr—"

"Katelyn!" The word is half strangled as it leaves her throat. "It's Katelyn. And if you speak my daughter's name again, I will call the police."

My eyes bug out. I wasn't sure, not until the moment my name left her lips. Gone is the locked jaw, the lifted chin. My heart isn't frozen; it's on fire. "Where's my mom?" My question is pleading—shaking, even.

"I don't know." She whips away from me, moving to the door, presumably to listen and make sure Grace hasn't heard anything. "I warned her a few times over the years, told her whenever they were getting close to finding her."

"Why?" Malcolm asks, speaking for the first time as if he knew I couldn't. "Why would you help your husband's mistress, the woman you just told us killed him?"

Instead of answering, Laura moves to a cabinet set against one wall. Opening the upper door, she reaches deep inside and pulls out a locked wooden box. Producing a key from her pocket, she unlocks it and lifts the lid before taking out a cell phone. It's small and simple, and the same brand as the disposable phone Mom left me with at the motel. "Here. I used this the last time I spoke with her, which was days ago. I don't have her number. It's always blocked, and she changes it constantly."

"You're the person she called that night," I say as the connection slams into me. I turn to Malcolm. "Before we ran, my mom made a call. I don't remember exactly what she said, but she was confirming that we needed to leave."

Laura doesn't deny it. "That's all I have. You can take the phone and go, or you can wait for the police to get here." She punctuates her threat by removing her own cell phone from her pocket, holding it as casually as someone would a weapon when up against an unarmed man.

And then her eye twitches.

I take the disposable phone and pass it to Malcolm without shifting my gaze from Laura. "Can you find her from this?" I ask him.

"Maybe. I need a computer."

I raise my eyebrows at Laura, whose slight frown is now the only indication that she's anything but calm.

"I don't have one in here." It's clear she wants that to be the end of the discussion, but it's just as clear that I've called her bluff. I know the word *accessory* as well as she does, and I'm happy to repeat it to the police we both know she won't call.

"There's a computer in the office." I can feel the ice in her stare as it bores into me, and I shiver. "Please do not make any noise that will bring my daughter downstairs."

I sink my teeth hard into my lip and nod. I heard Grace's voice. It's not enough, but it has to be right now. I get my mom *or* my sister. Laura won't give me both.

We follow her to another room, and Malcolm practically dives at the computer when he sees it.

"This is yours?" he asks with a note of awe. There are three monitors, and the entire setup looks impressive even to my untrained eye. I don't even recognize the logo embossed on the backs.

"My husband's. He's out of town."

191

"What does he do?" Malcolm's hands hover above the keyboard like he's afraid to touch it.

"Computer stuff" is the flat answer Laura gives him. I'm sure she could perfectly recite his job title and the parameters of his work, but she's determined to tell us as little as possible.

Malcolm nods, then flicks his gaze to me. "I can find her."

His words and the promise behind them help thaw the cold from Laura's glacial stare as Malcolm starts working.

"How did you find me?" she asks.

Without looking up from the computer screen, Malcolm raises a few fingers to claim his due.

"Computer stuff," I say, and her gaze snaps back to me. I take in the slight but noticeable tremble in her body. She's holding herself together by sheer force of will, and I'm suddenly, shamefully, reminded that she has every reason for acting the way she is. "I'm sorry," I add. "I wouldn't have come here if I had any other choice. I only just found out about . . . about everything. I didn't know about any of you." My gaze drifts upward. "I never dreamed I had a sister."

Like lightning, she crosses the room and seizes my upper arm in a grip so tight I cry out. The sound jerks Malcolm from his chair, ready to come to my aid if I need him. Laura leans in to me, her grip not loosening in the slightest.

"My daughter is nothing to you. Do you understand me? She is not *your* anything." Her teeth click together as she bites off the last word, and I flinch. "I can't call the police. From the very first, I made a choice that cut off that possibility for me.

192

But I will protect my daughter." Her fingers dig deeper, like she wants to crush the bone. Just as fast as the assault came, she releases me, and I'm the one left shaking. "You stay away from her."

My head is moving, nodding, agreeing to something I can't possibly agree to. I stop rubbing my arm the second I realize I'm doing it. I've never even laid eyes on my sister and I'm giving her up? Is this what my mom did, cower under the threat of this formidable woman?

And yet, *she's* afraid of *me*. I can see it in the way she's trying not to start whenever I shift my weight.

I remember the false fierceness I had to put on with Malcolm when we were first thrown together, the hardness I could only begin to play at, because the truth was that he terrified me.

I terrify Laura.

But why?

Grace has to know that her father died before she was born. She would have grown up in a world where her paternity wasn't a secret. She could have Googled him and watched the exact same news story I had, and so many more. She had to know who my mom was too, or at least who the police and press said she was. None of this would have been kept from her the way it had me. Grace isn't a child. She's older than me, almost nineteen. As for me personally, finding out about my existence might be a shock, but not the earth-shattering one that Laura is treating it as.

It doesn't make sense.

I'm missing something.

"Can I use your bathroom?" I say.

A burst of panic shows me the whites of her eyes. "The one on this floor is being remodeled."

That leaves upstairs. Where Grace is. Grace, who Laura wants me as far away from as possible.

In the end, she has no choice but to take me there. Malcolm is the lesser threat in her mind, and she isn't about to take her eyes off me.

This time, my gaze sweeps methodically over every inch of the tastefully decorated home: the cream paint, the subtle cornflower-blue accents, the plush white furniture. I'm not looking at the decor though; I'm looking for pictures. I don't see any on the way to the stairs, and none line the pin-striped wallpaper as we ascend to the second floor.

Laura moves slowly, cautiously, in front of me. Her shoulder blades are pulled so tightly together I think they might burst through the back of her cardigan. I can hear Grace—*we* can hear Grace—presumably in the bedroom at the end of the hall.

The door is only half closed, and if I lean all the way to the right, I can glimpse a sliver of her room. Her walls are purple, like a hazy sunrise that's still caught up in the night before. My heart beats faster. She'd hear me if I called out now. I wouldn't even have to yell.

But Laura is stopping, opening a door to a bathroom, and we're still a dozen feet from Grace's room. I hesitate, and Laura doesn't have to voice a threat. Every inch of her promises a lethal response if I fail to do exactly what I swore: keep quiet.

I cry in the bathroom, even though I'm close to finding my mom, closer than I've been since this nightmare began. My grandfather didn't know me. He screamed at me and was so lost in his past that he couldn't find the present. But Grace could know me.

I flush the toilet, because Laura is listening. Then I wash my hands and splash water on my face. I don't linger over my reflection. I don't recognize it anyway.

"Mom? What are you doing there?"

Grace. I reach for the door the second I hear her in the hall. But the handle doesn't turn. Laura is holding it from the other side. I can imagine her leaning back against it, blocking Grace's view so she won't see the handle fighting against her. I promised to be quiet, but nothing more.

"Hmm?" Laura says, sweetness and ease. "I was thinking about replacing the wallpaper up here. What do you think?"

Footsteps. I push harder on the handle. It doesn't give an inch.

"I like it the way it is," Grace says. There's something about her voice. Something I've heard before but can't place. "Why are you . . . Who's in the bathroom?"

There's no outward show of defeat when Laura finally releases the handle and lets me open the door. She even smiles at me as I nearly stumble into the hall.

PURSUE

"Grace, this is Katelyn. She and her friend stopped by to use your father's computer. Katelyn, this is my daughter, Grace."

I see her feet first, her sparkly turquoise-painted toes, her black yoga pants, and the loose, Doris Day T-shirt that I would kill to add to my collection.

And when I see her face, a piece falls into place.

"Hi, Katelyn."

She smiles at me, and I feel it. That instantaneous, shocking cementing of one person to another.

"Hi," I say back.

It's like I'm meeting every celebrity I've ever idolized all rolled into one. I can't take my eyes off her. We don't really look alike. Both of us favor our mothers more than our father in terms of coloring, but she has bangs like me and, as we stare at each other, we both lift our left hands to brush them from

196

our eyes at the same time. I laugh, and the sound turns watery. I don't think I've ever felt this much happiness. It should be radiating from my skin.

"Grace is a really pretty name," I tell her. And it's apparently the exact perfect thing to say, because she lights up.

"Grace was my great-grandmother's name. Do you want to see a picture of her?" She barely waits for me to nod before she takes my hand in hers and leads me to her room. She doesn't notice the distressed half squeak that escapes from her mother.

Grace's room is a mess, and I love it. It's how my room would look if I ever felt settled enough in one place to actually live in it. I spot a few books that I read growing up, in piles on the window seat, and makeup scattered atop a mirrored vanity. There's a robe tossed onto a white four-poster bed, and a fluffy orange cat lounging lazily atop it. Grace doesn't release my hand even when she brings us to a stop in front of a wall that is covered in framed photos.

"That's her." She pushes a short finger into the face of a striking woman who could have easily graced the silver screen. "And that's her again." The same woman, slightly older and gazing lovingly at a bundled baby in her arms. "And again, and again, and . . ." Her finger taps out an obviously well-rehearsed pattern as she traces her great-grandmother's life from some of its first moments to its last.

"She was beautiful," I say, staring at one of the earlier pictures, one Grace lingered over too. It's an older photograph, black and white, a bride on her wedding day. Grace's great-grandmother's hand is wrapped around her husband's, and the ring I've worn by my heart for years is on her finger.

"Mom's trying to get Grandmother Abbott to let me have Great-Grandma Grace's wedding dress, but Grandmother Abbott says it'd be a waste and I'd never fit in it anyway." This admission doesn't seem to bother Grace, or maybe she's grown so accustomed to hearing similar things that she no longer lets them affect her. Either way, I'd know which one Grace loved more. One has years of her smiling photos framed on Grace's walls, and the other is stiffly referred to as Grandmother Abbott.

"I don't have to wear it," Grace continues. "But to have it so I could see it sometime, I'd like that. I never met Great-Grandma Grace, but mom says she was nice, that she would have been nice to me. She would have let me stand next to her in photos and would never have called me"—I catch just enough of her mumbled words to make my ears burn hot and my fists clench—"defective . . . unsuitable . . ."

I can't even imagine someone saying such vile things to her own granddaughter.

Laura's arm slides protectively around her daughter. "Remember, we don't listen to the things Grandmother Abbott says. I'm taking care of everything. But now, I think it's time for Katelyn to leave. I'm sure her friend is waiting for her."

If I hadn't seen her face as she spoke, I'd never have known from Laura's voice that she was close to grabbing my hair and dragging me down the stairs. Another second and I think she would have.

"Grace, why don't you give Elvis his brushing. His fur looks a little tangled to me."

Concern flashes in Grace's eyes as she turns to her cat and moves to scoop him into her lap. The last sight I have of Grace is her snuggling his soft fur as he begins to purr.

Laura takes my arm again to lead me away, and her grip tightens with every step until we reach the foyer. Malcolm is standing there, looking like he wants to be anywhere else.

"Did you find her?" I no longer care about keeping my voice down. Laura shut Grace's door when we left. I almost want him to say no, that he needs more time, so I can go back upstairs with my sister, but his quick nod douses that hope.

"Then you need to leave." Laura swings the front door wide open, and all three of us are slapped with the wind and drizzling rain.

"How far?" I ask. Grace is walking around upstairs again. I bet she's getting the comb to brush her cat. Elvis. It's a cool name for a cat.

And Grandmother Abbott is a bitch.

Malcolm eyes Laura before answering, and I appreciate his discretion. "Close enough. But we can't walk."

Laura is staring at the dark sky outside. She blinks and breathes, then spins on her heel and walks to a narrow table just past the stairs. She returns and holds out a set of car keys. "I will report it stolen in the morning."

I start to take the keys, then stop. "You did it all for her, didn't you?"

The keys clink in Laura's hand.

"You knew even when you were pregnant. Did Derek?"

I shake my head, because it doesn't matter. Grace would have always been the legitimate heir, even if I'd showed up at some point, but Laura must have learned enough about her in-laws while she was pregnant to know that given the choice between a legitimate heir born with Down syndrome and an illegitimate one born without . . . they'd have rejected Grace.

I felt carved-out and slick with nausea. Grandmother Abbott's disdain for Grace wasn't a secret even from her. I'm ready to gag on the disgust I feel for a woman I've never met.

"That's why you helped my mom all these years, so she'd stay hidden and keep me hidden too."

Clink, clink, clink.

"I don't want anything from his family," I say. "I just want my mom. Grace is . . . She's . . ." Laura won't want to hear anything from me about her daughter. I spent all of five minutes with her, but I don't even hesitate as I reach behind my neck and undo the clasp of my necklace. I coil up the chain along with the ring and set it atop the banister. "Grace should have this."

I take the car keys, and Malcolm and I step out into the rain. The second Laura shuts the door, I turn to him.

"I met her," I say. "Grace. She was sweet, so sweet. And I hate my mother right now. I hate her. And Laura. And most of all, I hate my grandmother."

Malcolm is missing crucial pieces that would allow him to understand everything I'm saying, but he doesn't hurl any questions at me; he runs a hand over my hair and cradles my head.

"You really found her?" I ask him.

"I found where she was three days ago." His arms tighten around me, as though he's trying to support me for what he says next. "I don't know if she's still there. And, um, she wasn't trying to hide. Not like a woman who's spent nearly two decades avoiding capture. It was like she wanted someone to be able to follow her."

I bite down on the inside of my cheek, thinking about the risk she's been taking. If they'd still had Malcolm, they'd have found her long before I could. "She was drawing them away from me," I say with certainty. "And I know she's still there. She's been waiting for this. It's my birthday at midnight. And now I know exactly why she had to wait till I'm eighteen. Whatever else Laura warned my mom about, keeping Grandmother Abbott as far away from me as possible was highest on that list. She's planning to turn herself in."

The clock inside said it was almost nine o'clock. In three hours, I'll be safe. And Mom will be . . .

Gently, I free myself from Malcolm's embrace. "Let's go."

I'm not reeling from shock and a concussion like I was the last time I pulled into a motel parking lot. I'm alert and focused, and fear has been my companion for so long that I've forgotten how it feels to be in any other state. Except now excitement is also tripping through me, and something like desperation.

"Katelyn." Malcolm lays a hand on my arm. "Why don't you let me go first? It'll probably freak her out if she opens her door and sees you."

I soak in the warmth from his hand and try less successfully to draw comfort from his words. He's trying to protect me from what he believes might devastate me. He's not so sure my mom is safe and sound inside the motel he tracked her to, watching the clock. I get that, but I can't believe it. "She's fine, and so am I. You'll see."

The car door shutting behind me brings the entire motel into hyperfocus. It's a large two-story L-shaped building with red doors and a matching roof. There are several other cars in the parking lot besides ours, and I note them all without meaning to, another game Mom and I played whenever we went to a restaurant. She'd let me get dessert whenever I could correctly recite the description of every car in the parking lot.

It's been five days since I saw her. Only five days. It feels longer, like an eternity. I know she's inside.

I could never have anticipated the last week. It's fair to

assume that Mom's plans impacted with reality in ways she couldn't have guessed either, but she's okay. I hate that I have to keep telling myself that, but I do. I keep it up for every step until I'm standing outside room 7A.

The rain has stopped and the Do Not Disturb sign is hanging on the door, swaying back and forth in the same breeze that lifts my dark-brown hair into my line of vision. I take a minute to smooth it back, tucking it neatly behind my ears and tugging my sweater down in a vain attempt to make it fit better. That's all the repair I can make to my appearance here; it'll have to be enough.

My hand hovers over the door but doesn't move. Something thick is in my throat, and the wind catches my eyes at just the right angle to make them sting and water.

And then I knock.

REUNITE

There is no answer, so I try again, rapping the metal door with a force that approaches painful. I don't stop, can't imagine ever stopping, until the door disappears under my hand.

The force of the red door swinging open blows my hair back, and it's her. She's standing there, eyes wide, with a knife in her hand.

Flinching is instinctual, as is crossing my arms in front of my face, until . . .

"Katelyn!"

The blunt side of the knife presses into my spine as she surges forward and wraps her arms around me, only to jerk back just as quickly, leaving the hand with the knife on my shoulder. Her eyes, if possible, go even wider, and she shakes me once.

"You can't be here. Not now." She pulls me into the room

with the same strength she used to scale our neighbor's fence, then slams the door shut behind me. She opens her mouth, then closes it, hugs me again, softer this time, and almost buries her words in my hair. "You're supposed to be so far away."

I hold her, soaking up her body heat and ignoring the slight sour scent of sweat on her skin. For all my confidence with everyone else, I wasn't sure I'd ever get to do this again: See her and hug her. Feel safe.

But that feeling is fleeting and wholly insufficient in the face of so much deception. I pull her to sit on the edge of the bed with me. "I found my grandfather," I say.

I don't ask why she didn't tell me he was still alive. Everything is tangled up together. Revealing one piece would have involved divulging the whole. I might not agree with her decision to keep all this from me, but I understand her reasoning.

"I saw the sonogram picture, and I know Derek Abbott is my father."

Mom goes stiff at this.

"And then I went to see Laura."

Her back snaps tight.

"I also met my half sister. She doesn't know who I am, but I talked to her. She has a cat named Elvis." My voice turns harsh. "And you *kept her* from me."

Mom stands and takes two deliberate steps away, her back to me. "I know."

"That's it?" A dizziness begins to buzz in my head, making

me grateful that I'm sitting. I see her shoulders start to tremble, matching my voice. "You lied about my entire life. My grandfather, my sister. Who my father was, and the fact that you're accused of killing him!"

Mom looks at me from over her shoulder, her eyes brimming with tears, but she says nothing.

"Say something!"

Her voice is a whisper. "I can't."

"You can, but you won't. You don't know what I've been through these past few days, what I've had to do." My voice chokes on the last word.

She starts to turn her body toward me, pauses in the act to breathe through her nose, then turns the rest of the way. "You were supposed to stay at the motel, where you were safe. I could have explained everything once it was over."

"Safe? No, Mom, there is no safe." I suck in a deep breath. "They found me at the motel."

I tell her about the bounty hunter chasing me through the woods, how I hid from him under a bed, disguised myself, ran from a cop, and found my grandfather, only to end up locked in a pitch-dark room waiting for a painful interrogation that I didn't stick around for.

"You did good." She takes my face firmly in her hands. "You did the exact right thing."

I pull away. "I had no choice, because you left me alone." Still standing close to her, I take in her wan appearance: the limp and unwashed hair, the scrape along her jaw, the dark smudges under her eyes. She looks like she's been through at least as much as I have. But then my eyes drop lower. She's not standing right, even though she's trying to hide it.

"Mom?"

She doesn't answer, but her eyes shift away so deliberately that I feel compelled to look in the opposite direction.

At first, all I see is the unmade bed, which in and of itself would raise warning flags. Mom would make her bed while sick with the flu, even if she had to take puke breaks while doing it. That's not hyperbole; she's literally done that before. But then I see the crumpled-up coverlet hastily thrown over the mattress, nearly but not completely hiding the stains underneath. Some are red, others rust brown. As I pull back the sheet, larger splotches come into view.

When I turn back to her, the pretense is gone. She's got one arm braced on her knee, and she's leaning heavily against the dresser with the other.

"It's not bad," she says, her taut lips belying her words. "I thought I had time when I left you and went somewhere I shouldn't have. Someone was watching, and I sliced my thigh open getting away."

I'm at her side in half a heartbeat, helping her to the edge of the bed; she can't hide her grimace when she sits. It's worse when I roll up her loose pant leg to expose the makeshift bandage she'd applied and secured with duct tape.

A washcloth is crusted to her skin with dried blood, and I have to run another one under the faucet in the bathroom to work the edges free. I can feel her studying me, my hair, my hands, connecting what dots she can as I work the bandage free. She lets me do all this in silence, leaning back to give me better access. When I peel the final side off, it reveals a deep gash running from above her knee all the way to her midthigh.

I see yellow fat.

If it were any deeper, I'd see bone.

I choke and bring my hand to my mouth. Our roles reverse, and suddenly she's the one comforting me.

"It's okay," she says. "It looks worse than it is."

Another lie. She's told me enough over the course of my life that I'm beginning to recognize them.

I tape a fresh washcloth back over her thigh. "This is why you didn't call, isn't it?" I say. "You knew they were going to catch up with you. You wanted to lead them away from me."

"I thought it was the police again. I didn't know until I left you, until they found me at the cemetery." She gestures at her thigh. "I realized I couldn't risk contacting you without endangering your life more than I already had."

"Derek's grave? You went to say goodbye to him." Heat sears up my neck. "And then, what, you were heading straight to the police station? Is that how you were going to keep your promise to tell me everything? From behind bars?"

She reaches for me, but I jerk away and I see her flinch like I slapped her.

I feel like I'm locked in a flooding room. My neck is craned back as high as possible while the rising water laps at my jaw, leaving me time for one last breath before I'm submerged and trapped.

"Did you do it?" I say. "Did you kill him?"

"Baby, it's complicated."

"No, Mom, it's not. The world says you're a killer. My grandfather still thinks you're a teenager. But he swears Derek was going to marry you. His actual wife at the time says you killed him. But then how could she help you? Either you killed a man for rejecting you or he was planning to leave his pregnant wife for you when he found out about me, and . . . what? Someone else killed him? His whole family decided to band together and blame you, and you've kept silent all these years letting them?"

The questions limp from my mouth. I don't ask them because I'm compelled to hear the answers; I'd ask the same things in a room by myself. But with nothing else to stop the rising water, I say, "Tell me the truth. I can't take another lie."

STANDOFF

"And that would be enough for you, my say-so?" Mom angles her head at me, the lightly chiding gesture so familiar it aches. "Would you really believe me if I said I didn't kill him?"

I open my mouth to shout yes. I can already feel my body swaying toward her—to hug her, hold her, and let her tell me it's all going to be okay. I'll believe her, anything she says, because I want this to be over more than I want the actual truth. I want it gone: the fear, the doubt, the sick uncertainty. I want my mom back.

My heart tears open. "Just say the words. Tell me you didn't kill him."

"My real name isn't Melissa Reed. It's Tiffany Jablonski. Your real father wasn't Anthony Reed. It was Derek Abbott. Your grandfather isn't dead, and you have a sister. You're not even the age you think you are. Did you know that?"

My chin quivers as I stare at her. "Why are you doing this?" I say. I've seen her face every day of my life; I know it better than my own. Without consciously meaning to, I take her hand. It's the same one that stroked my head as a child when nightmares chased me from sleep. The same hand that smeared green paint on every visible inch of my skin when I decided I wanted to be a gecko for Halloween. The same hand that held mine when we hiked the last mile in the Smoky Mountains a few months before.

She can't tell me she killed him. She can't tell me she didn't.

All the lies. So many.

The soft knock on the door momentarily startles me but sends her into kill-or-be-killed mode. She pushes me roughly to the floor and has the knife back in her hand all in the same motion.

"Katelyn?" Malcolm calls. "Are you okay?"

She whirls on me as I stand, a million silent questions in her eyes.

"It's okay. He's a friend. He's the one who helped me find you." When my words don't have the desired effect, I add, "He saved my life, and yours too."

She lowers the knife infinitesimally, and I open the door to let Malcolm in. He sees the knife right off and halts with one foot in the room.

"It's okay," I say to both of them. "She cut up her leg, but she's fine. I told you she would be."

He lifts his head in a half nod, acknowledging what I said but unable to tear his eyes away from the knife my mom is pointing at him.

"Please give me that," I say to her, but she's equally focused on Malcolm and barely listening. "Mom." That gets her attention. The knife trembles, and her eyes slide to me. "This is Malcolm." I take a slight step in front of him before ripping off the Band-Aid. "My grandmother hired him to find you."

⟁

Just like I kept my makeshift blade from the motel room tight in my hand for hours after meeting Malcolm, Mom is slow to fully release her knife. I coax her into a chair and run through the details of discovering Malcolm and then the two of us escaping together, dwelling on the initial injuries Malcolm sustained to give Mom and me a chance, and later his dogged insistence on helping me find her even after I gave him an out. I think I mostly succeed at convincing her he's not a threat, but she does insist that I leave the knife within easy reach of her.

The first thing she asks him is "Where'd you leave Laura's car?"

"At an apartment building two blocks down the road," he says. Then to me in a lower voice: "I assumed everything was okay when I saw her let you in."

I nod, silently thanking him both for the privacy he gave us and the foresight to ditch the car some distance from the motel.

"He should go," she says, then, with a slight eye roll that seems directed at herself, "You should too."

"Where would I go?" I ask. "Back to my cell at the bounty hunter's place?"

She doesn't answer, because she has no answer.

"Whatever you were planning to do, it's over now," I say. "You're not leaving me alone again."

Mom's gaze slides to mine at the steel in my voice. "I'm done running," she says, matching my tone.

"You're also done making unilateral decisions. I'm eighteen now, remember? Or I will be in a couple hours. I get a say. And since you can barely stand without breaking into a sweat, it's gonna be a big one." I have no idea what we're going to do in the long term, but the short term is obvious. "First up is your leg. You should have gone to the hospital days ago." I suppress a flare of queasiness remembering the red streaks emanating from the wound.

"She can't go to the hospital," Malcolm says.

I round on him, shocked that he isn't taking my side. "That's the only place she can go. Her leg is bad: it looks infected, and she's lost a lot of blood. She's going."

He takes a few cautious steps toward Mom and me, the way you'd approach a snarling animal. Which is exactly what I feel like. "The investigator knows she's here somewhere, and that she's hurt."

He glances at Mom for confirmation, and she nods.

"Okay, then they probably have people at all the nearby hospitals waiting for her to come in."

The ground opens up to swallow me. He's right.

"Malcolm," I say, lowering my voice and moving toward him. "She needs help. She needed it days ago. I just got her back. I can't even think about—"

"I know. We'll help her."

"*You'll* do nothing," Mom says.

I don't miss the emphasis on *you'll*, or the way her eyes are locked on the spot where Malcolm rests his hand on me. Not wanting her to waste any energy worrying about *that*, I shift away from him. "Malcolm's proven himself to me. You're just going to have to take my word for it."

She hasn't spared more than a glance for him since I made her lower her knife. I can't forget how alike we are. The strength of her animosity toward Malcolm will be at least as intense as mine was initially, and she doesn't have the luxury of time to assuage it.

She shifts her gaze to him, narrowing her eyes as though trying to make a decision. Then she takes a shuffled step to the side, and her injured leg gives out.

Malcolm is closer than I am. He leaps to catch her and helps her to the bed. He grunts as his ribs bear her weight.

"I'm okay," she says. "I moved too fast."

"You've lost too much blood."

Her eyes slowly close, then open halfway. "Just give me a minute, okay? Then we'll talk. We'll figure everything out together. Go clean up. I think I got blood on your sweater."

I reach for Malcolm's hand, because I can't take hers. I'm afraid I'll crush it. This moment is the worst yet. She looks so frail, weak.

Hurt.

"Okay," I say, miraculously keeping my voice steady. "Call out if you need something." Her eyes are already drifting shut again.

Malcolm follows me to the bathroom and lets me close the door behind him. The space is slightly larger than a phone booth. I place a finger to my lips and lean past him to turn on the water in the sink to full blast. I would turn on the shower, but Mom would never be so faint as to let the notion of me and a boy and a running shower go unnoticed, no matter how hurt she was. I whisper instead.

"I don't know what to do. She needs a doctor." I feel dizzy looking at the bloodied towels piled up in the bathroom. I put Lady Macbeth to shame scouring my hands clean of Mom's blood before starting in on the sweater. When my intense scrubbing threatens to add my own blood into the mix, I release the hem of my sweater and force my hands apart to brace on the sides of the sink. Lifting my eyes, I find Malcolm staring at me in the mirror.

"You gonna tell me what she said?"

"She didn't say anything." I squeeze the porcelain. "I'm the one who talked. I told her all the lies I'd unraveled, and she didn't deny any of them or offer excuses, but when I asked her point-blank if she killed Derek, she"—my voice goes tight—"she basically asked me how I could believe her if she told me she was innocent."

Malcolm is leaning against the wall behind me, his hands shoved into his pockets.

"I just don't know anymore. I don't know. I don't know if I want to know," I whisper. Not because Mom might hear me, but because I'm afraid to hear myself. It's my confession, the one that's been steadily gaining ground on me for longer than I'll admit. I focus on the reflection of Malcolm's honey-brown eyes locked on mine. "And I know that's not what I promised you."

"No," he says just as softly before pulling his mouth to the side in half a sneer. "You know it's not like that anymore."

"That's not fair," I tell him. "You're here because of me, hurt because—"

He pushes off from the wall and tugs at a loop of my jeans to turn me around so we're face to face. His hand stays warm and solid on my hip. "What'd you say to me that first night when you kept that window edge tight in your hand whenever I so much as breathed at you wrong?"

He's so close that I have to lift my head to meet his gaze. "I said a lot of things I wish I hadn't."

His lips curl up slightly. "I'm not talking about all the threats. You told me that ignorance isn't the same as innocence. I got caught in this because of me, I got hurt because of some sadistic bastard with steel-toed boots, but I did decide to stay because of you." He lifts his hand, and his thumb lightly brushes the cut under my bangs, leaving a trail of warmth behind. "Because the only one who's truly been innocent in all of this is you."

Had I really ever been afraid of him? That emotion feels a million miles away from the one tingling through my skin and radiating through my chest. It's almost enough to block out the chill stealing through the cracks around the window and the shadows creeping in under the door from the dark room outside.

Almost.

I curl my fingers around his wrist and lower his hand from my face. "If I'm innocent, why do I feel so guilty?"

"So we're asking church questions now." Then he steps away, giving me as much room as the bathroom will allow. It's not much, but it's worlds easier to breathe in here than in the room with my mom. "It was the same with my dad. He made all these promises to me and Gran after he got out of prison the first time. Said he was going to be there for me, show me how to be a man, that kind of stuff. Sang on Sundays louder than anybody. And afterward, when those same patterns started coming back, it was like as long as I never looked, never asked, he didn't have to be a liar." His hands return to his pockets. "But when they came for him again, when it all came out, I was the one left feeling like a criminal."

The cold sink behind me is jarring after Malcolm's touch.

"I'm not saying that's you or it's the same. I'm saying I understand not wanting to know. I still wish I didn't."

"But isn't that worse? Was it any better when you found out?"

His eyes go soft, so soft. "I don't know. I didn't get to choose with my dad. And," he says, "he wasn't like your mom. He stole for himself, for the thrill."

"But that's what I don't know. Tiffany Jablonski and Melissa Reed. All this time, has she been running from something or for something?"

His smile doesn't reach his eyes. "From the second I met you, you never doubted her love. Maybe she ran at first from her mistakes, but you're the reason she kept running."

Something bright fills my chest at that. Not just from his smile, which is sunshine after the rain, but from the truth I recognize in his words. My mom's always done whatever it took to keep me safe. I learned that from her. Even now, she—

Malcolm's smile vanishes as I push past him and yank the door open.

The bed is empty. Mom's gone.

SEARCH

"She conned me," I say, my voice softened by disbelief. Not about being hurt, but about how weak she was. She didn't need to lie down; she needed to make me think she was giving in, so that she could take off.

Malcolm hurries past me to look outside, but I don't join him. I know she's already gone. I check for the keys to Laura's car and find them still safely tucked in my back pocket. That only means we're not stuck here. Mom will get herself a car if she hasn't already.

Malcolm is slow in returning. "I didn't see her."

"How many vehicles were in the parking lot?"

He has to duck back out to count before telling me, "Eleven."

"There were twelve when we got here." I also knew that there were exactly sixteen rooms, and nine of those had Do Not Disturb signs hanging from their doors.

"So she took one?"

219

"Probably. Maybe she even got the owner to give it to her." Glancing outside myself, I register that a white Nissan pickup is missing. I stand there, trying to figure out what she's doing.

Malcolm paces. "You still think she's going to turn herself in?"

"I mean, I thought that was her plan. Wait till I'm eighteen so social services or whoever can't come after me. But then why—"

"Run?"

I nod and sink onto the corner of the bed. "We could have all stayed here together, and she could have called the police in . . ." I twist around to see the alarm clock on the nightstand. "In an hour. She could have explained everything and never had to go through the investigator or his people, if that's what was keeping her from the hospital. I don't understand." I run my hand over the crumpled polyester bedspread. In disarray, just like the rest of the room. And it stinks. It smells sour and faintly coppery from the blood. There's an empty bottle of painkillers and some protein bar wrappers in the trash. Not a lot, but a few. She hasn't had much of an appetite.

I can see her over the past few days, hiding here the way she thought I was hiding safely a state away, waiting. I drag my toe over the worn carpet and imagine her pacing around the bed. She chews her nails just like I do. I wonder if she imposed the same rules on herself that she did on me: no peeking out windows, no leaving the room, no phone calls. Another glance at the nightstand confirms that she didn't yank the phone cord out of the wall. But she had a cell phone. She called Laura even if she didn't call me. She could have called anyone. . . .

Rising to my feet, I stride over to Mom's left-behind bag and upend it on the floor. Clothes, shoes, and a few toiletries spill out, and not much else. I turn my head to Malcolm and rise from my squat.

Malcolm, still pacing, stops midstride. "What? What are you thinking?"

"How long do you think we were in the bathroom?" I start methodically moving around the room to check drawers.

"Five minutes maybe. Why?"

"Even still, she wouldn't have known that." I check the mini fridge, the microwave. "For all she knew, we'd be back out in less than one."

"Okaaaaay," Malcolm says.

"So she must have bolted the second we closed the bathroom door." I'm removing picture frames from walls, tossing pillows and blankets. "She wouldn't have had time to take anything. Look." I nod my head toward the nightstand. "She didn't even grab the knife."

Malcolm starts picking things up, joining me in the search. "What am I looking for?"

"Her phone."

He looks under the bed corners, and I remove the lid to the toilet tank. We unscrew the air vents, and Malcolm even

thinks to unzip the chair cushions. But all we find is dust bun-
nies and liberally stained foam. The phone has to be close and
easily accessible, in case she had to run again. Plus with her
injury, it's not like she dug a hole or buried it outside. It's in this
room somewhere. Nowhere else makes sense.

I turn to watch Malcolm pry up a corner of carpet. He isn't
looking at me, so I smile. I can tell he'll keep searching with me
until the very last second.

Empty-handed, he finally pushes to his feet.

"What's left?"

He rubs a hand over his head. "The ceiling maybe, somehow? She had a knife." He gestures toward it. "She could have
used it to unscrew the light fixture and . . ."

"Climb up on a chair with *her* leg?"

He doesn't say anything about how ridiculous that sounds;
he just shrugs and pulls a chair under the light.

She would need someplace low, maybe even someplace she
could reach sitting down—or, better yet, lying down. He's right
about the knife, though. If she could cut into something . . .

And just like that, I know.

It must show on my face, because Malcolm halts with one
foot on the chair as I practically dive under the bed.

"We looked there, remember?"

But I'm not searching under the bed. I'm looking up, at the
box spring, and yes, the lining is cut.

I'm turning the phone on to toss to Malcolm before I've

even crawled back out. "Please tell me there's a call log and you recognize a number."

"Laura's number, Laura's number, Laura's number—"

"That one." Crowded beside him, shoulder to shoulder, I jam my finger against the tiny screen as a new number appears. "She called that number . . . right before we got here. That has to be where she went, right?"

One glance up at Malcolm's suddenly blank expression, and I know he recognizes it. "Who? Malcolm, tell me."

"That's Mrs. Abbott's number."

APPROACH

The Abbott estate is set back nearly a mile from the road. We can't even see the house through all the trees when we pull up to the gated entry. Malcolm groans before he kills the engine. "I don't know if I can scale another wall."

"You don't have to," I say as I unbuckle my seat belt.

His head snaps to me. "I'm not sending you in there alone."

I find a smile for him somewhere in all my panic for Mom. "No, I mean you don't have to climb over. Neither of us does. Look." I point to the white Nissan pickup some twenty yards away. It's parked right up against the wall. "Mom wasn't scaling anything either. You'll still have to jump down, but I can catch you if you want."

"Hey," he says as I turn to open my door. When I glance back over my shoulder, he fits his hand to my chin. "Apologies to your not-boyfriend, but—" And then Malcolm kisses me.

It's fast and hard and I barely have time to close my eyes before it's over, but it's maybe the best kiss of my life.

"In case you drop me or something and lose that flicker of attraction you've had since I kicked you the first time we met."

We're still really close, inches apart. So close that I can see that his eyes are flecked with gold.

"You never apologized for that."

"What do you think I just did?" That soft look in his eyes fades when he adds, "Now let's go find your mom."

Jumping down from the wall hurts. And Malcolm refuses to let me catch him, opting instead to accept my hand when he botches the landing and slips on some wet leaves.

"Okay?" I ask when he's standing again. He glares at me in answer. No, he's not okay, but it doesn't matter. Like he said in the car, he's not sending me in alone. I should probably be frustrated with his stubbornness, but I'm too relieved.

We move up the driveway as quickly and cautiously as we can. It curves around a pond at one point and branches off toward a pool and a guesthouse at another. The moon is bright and nearly full, but there are so many trees lining the property—lofty sycamores, maples, and evergreens—that we never have to stray from the shadows. The air is damp and cold, and my goose bumps have goose bumps before we finally see the main house.

Towering before us are three stories of light-gray stone, with arching windows and walls of glass, all covered with heavy drapes. It doesn't look like a home so much as a mausoleum. That chilling thought brings me up short, because that's exactly what it is. My father—my real father—died here.

My mother fled down this exact driveway that night, and she walked back up it maybe ten minutes ago.

I don't know Mom's mindset or her intentions, but I can't imagine her brazenly knocking on the door. I start circling the house in search of an entrance. Mom wouldn't have wanted to walk any farther than she already had, and judging by the car she didn't bother hiding at the gate, she wasn't planning to slip in and out unnoticed. My heart lodges high in my throat. I don't think she's planning to get out at all.

Where, where, where would she have gone in? I'm not looking up. She's hurt; she needed someplace low. And she didn't have time. She knew I'd come after her, and if I found her once I could do it again.

It's the blood that tips me off. A basement window is broken, and glittering on one jagged edge is a smear of red. Relief isn't the emotion that hits me; it's more like intense panic, making me forget myself and call to Malcolm.

I have to break out more of the glass before I can wriggle through, and I still end up catching my sweater and slicing through a good chunk of my forearm. Malcolm has a much easier go of it, what with my blood, and Mom's, signaling the side to avoid.

"You okay?" he asks.

"Yeah." The cut is long, but I don't think it's deep. The adrenaline coursing through my body isn't letting me feel pain at the moment, though, so I don't really know if it's bad or not.

I tear off the strip of sweater the window started unraveling, and Malcolm helps me tie it over my cut arm. The need to find Mom is jittering through me so strongly that it's almost impossible to stand still, so as soon as he's done, I dash to a narrow set of steps and up to the first floor.

Faint light shows us another staircase, this one immense, bringing a formal sitting room into view along with a stacked stone fireplace so big I could stand in it. Moonlight reflects off a marble countertop far in the distance, in what is presumably the kitchen, but neither Malcolm nor I move in that direction.

Because above us we can hear voices.

And one of them belongs to my mother.

REPAY

The voices grow louder as we tiptoe up the stairs, and my pounding heart thumps with increasing intensity. For the first time since my mom left me, I'm at war between wanting to sprint toward something and wanting to flee from it.

There are no lights on in the long hallway at the top. The only source of illumination bleeds out from beneath a partially closed door at the end. Mom's voice is steady as we draw near, strong and sure.

"—what you wanted."

"What I wanted?" another voice says, an older woman, and I know by the way the hairs rise on the back of my neck that it belongs to my grandmother. "I want my son back."

"He was never going to do what you wanted, be what you wanted," my mom says. "*I'm* proof of that."

"You're only proof that he was afflicted by the same weakness his father was. And just like his father, he would have thrown you over the second he realized what his philandering would cost him."

We've crept close enough that I can peer into the room and see a sliver of the scene inside. My mother's back is to me, and dark red drops are shining wet on the gleaming wooden floor behind her. The trail leads back to the door Malcolm and I are hiding behind, and beneath our feet. It becomes hard to breathe when I think about the blood. I wanted to believe it came from cutting herself the way I had on the broken window, but she had to have been bleeding long before that. Jumping down from the wall alone would have torn open her already-injured leg, and the trek to the house must have been agony. She was wearing a jacket at the motel, but instead of cinching it around her thigh to help staunch the wound, she's tied it around her waist, to hide just how badly she's bleeding.

My grandmother, a trim woman who looks to be in her early seventies, rises to her feet behind a heavy oak desk. She has sleek silvery-blond hair turned under at her shoulders and held back in a headband that matches her blouse. A pair of reading glasses hangs from a delicate chain around her neck, the only visible concession to her age. "Now," she says with quiet menace, "give me the ring."

"I don't have it," Mom says, and my hand automatically flies to my chest, seeking the ring I no longer had, the one I'd left for my sister.

"That's a lie." Soft, smooth-looking cheeks that might even dimple if she smiled, quiver. "You'd never sell it."

"Because you know I loved him."

"Because you're a fool who believed a foolish boy."

"Is that what you think?" Mom half whispers. "That Derek lied to me? He gave me that ring."

"It wasn't his to give! When Mr. Abbott's mother died after Derek and Laura were already married, it was understood that the ring would be given to their daughter. Only Laura gave birth to"—her lips curl back—"an unsuitable child, so now it belongs to me."

Between the pain and my grandmother's nasty words, I have no idea how my mom is still upright. Only when watching closely can I see the faint trembling in her left leg, which she's forcing to bear all the weight from her right. But she's not panting that I can hear. She's standing like the house itself would fall before she would.

"I never wanted it, couldn't wear it without drawing attention. But he told me that his grandmother was the only kind person to ever come from the Abbott line and that we were going to change that. Our child would change that."

"Your child." Mrs. Abbott scoffs. "You never got to . . ." Her mouth stills, and her eyes, previously narrowed, drift open and distant. "No," she says. "He can't have been that foolish."

"I wanted to name her Grace after her great-grandmother, but Derek . . ." Mom's shaking increases in intensity. "I know now why he didn't."

A tear slips down my cheek.

"You—you—"

"Her name is Katelyn, and she is magnificent. And you"—my mom leans forward—"will never play a role in her life."

"Where is she?"

I can't see her face, but I imagine my mother is smiling.

"Where is she?" my grandmother repeats, so loudly this time that Malcolm and I both start. "You took my son from me. You will not take the only good part of him I have left."

I think of my sister and the utter disdain this woman has for her, and grind my teeth together.

"I didn't take him from you."

"You're the reason he's dead. He ran after you, and you pushed him—"

"I was trying to get away!" Mom half stumbles a step forward. "To make him let go. I was at the top of the stairs, and he had ahold of my arms. And when I jerked them free, he—he—" Mom's voice chokes off, sobs racking her body.

"No, no, you don't get to cry for him. You took him, ruined him, and you don't get to cry. Is that what you came here for? Forgiveness? If so, you're a greater fool than he was."

It feels like it takes ages for Mom to stop crying, to pull herself back from that night, and I see the effort it's costing her. I see so much, and I see it in ways I haven't before. The life she already gave up to save mine. The years of running and hiding that fact from me so I wouldn't have to grow up scared. I see the way she kept my father near me as best she could, the only way she thought she could. I see the normal life she tried to give me, I see the lengths she has gone to and the ones she's still going to. For me.

She may not be crying now, but I am.

"I only want the truth," she says. "Not for the world, I don't care about them. I'll tell the police whatever you want, confess to anything. I want the truth for my daughter, for Derek's daughter. He was a coward who couldn't stand up to his parents when they forced him into a marriage he never wanted, but he loved Katelyn from the moment he knew she existed, and he loved me too. You know that. Tell her the truth, and I'll stop running."

"You're already done running," my grandmother says, reaching to open a drawer beside her. "My husband may not have lived long enough to see this day, but we both knew how it would end. Not with confessions, not with police, but with justice."

The small gun she points at my mother is black, and so matte it seems to suck light. And I'm screaming, barreling into the room, promising the ring and myself and anything else my fear-frozen brain can think of.

But it's too late.

My grandmother gasps at me, arm slipping, and fires at my mother in that single breath.

SHOT

I become nothing as the bullet hits my mom.

There's no sound.

No sight.

No senses at all.

I push forward as though I'm moving through wet cement. I'm running, but the air pushes back. It won't give, won't let me reach her.

And she's falling backward, her hair floating up to hide her face, her arms drifting forward.

Fire.

It starts in my throat, tearing from my lungs, piercing my ears.

Screaming.

I'm screaming.

She hits the ground, and I'm miles away, so far away. I see her skull thud against the wood floor, see it push her back up so that she slams down a second time.

I slip.

I slip on her blood.

Blood from her leg, which had been pooling while she traded her freedom so that I would know I was loved.

Blood that gurgles up from high on her chest and trickles down over her shoulder.

I'm hurting her, I have to be hurting her, when I reach her, grab her. "Mom. Mom. Mommommommom."

"It's okay," she says. She's still lying to me. I can feel her lies sticky and wet on my hands. "It hit my shoulder, Katelyn. Look."

I look, but all I see is blood.

Mom's short, sharp breaths come into focus. Sneakers thudding across the floor, squeaking and skidding. A lamp crashing to the floor.

My grandmother yelling.

Malcolm grunting.

And a second shot.

BLEED

This time, there is sound.

The clatter of the gun as it falls to the ground.

The thud from Malcolm's body hitting the floor.

The cry from my grandmother as he nearly takes her down with him.

Malcolm rolls his head toward me, and I see a dribble of blood escape from the corner of his mouth.

Blood. I'm drowning in it, and it's almost as though I can taste it flooding my own throat. I'm choking on it.

Mom's hand finds mine and she seizes it, forcing my attention to her. "Call 9-1-1."

I lunge for the landline phone that Malcolm and my grandmother sent crashing to the floor when he tried to take the gun from her. I grab the handset and use it to tug the base toward me. I'm cradling it to my chest as I scramble to reach Malcolm.

"It's going to be okay," I tell him even as his blood starts to soak into my jeans. "You're fine. I'm going to get help." I fumble to right the base in my lap with one hand, since my other is wadding up a throw blanket from a small couch and pressing it against the wound at his side.

I jam at buttons and listen to the ringing, ringing, ring—

Silence.

My grandmother stands by the wall, the ripped-out phone cord hanging from her hand.

"No," she says. "That's not how this ends. He stays right there. He broke in with your mother, and they attacked me." Her light-blue eyes grow clearer as she speaks. "She'll go to prison this time, both for killing my son and attempting to kill me. She realized how close the investigation was getting and decided to come after me, seeking revenge for a life forcibly lived in the shadows. My investigator was here when they broke in; he witnessed everything, so he can corroborate my statement to the police." Malcolm coughs up more blood. "Of course, he'll have to die," she adds, glancing at him. "But that shouldn't take long."

My limbs turn to ice. "You can't—*I'm* here. I saw what happened." But even as I speak, the doubts creep in. Not about the truth, but about who will believe it. My mother was condemned because of the story the Abbots spun, and Malcolm could be all too easily painted with the same brush as his father. If the investigator will lie for my grandmother, together they can make this night look like whatever they want. It'll be my tainted word against theirs.

Malcolm will bleed out on the floor. I'll lose Mom.

The gun is in my hand before I consciously decide to reach for it. I'm trembling so badly that I can barely keep it aimed at the woman threatening to take everything from me.

I expect the protests, the pleas, when they come, but not from my mom.

"No, Katelyn. No."

I'm still staring at my grandmother's ashen face when I answer my mom. "If she dies, then we can run again, hide again. I can call for help for Malcolm, and we can leave. It'll be better this time, because I'll know. I won't mess up, and I can help." My finger slides to the trigger. It's still warm. My hand steadies. "I won't let her take you."

"Look at me. Right now." Mom's not yelling or even raising her voice. She's calm and all the more compelling for it. I tear my gaze away from my grandmother and look to where my mother is pushing herself up into a sitting position. Her features pull tight as she moves, but her voice betrays none of the pain she must be in. "I have lived your entire life with a death on my conscience."

"But you didn't mean for him to die. It was an accident."

"That was the worst night of my life. Seeing them, seeing *her*. And he didn't defend me, just let me stand there crying as his mother . . ." She shudders. "It was too late when he tried to come after me, apologizing for being a coward who wasn't free to be with the person he loved. I couldn't think, couldn't see. I actually thought I might lose you that night, because I felt like

I was dying. And I pushed him. Not to hurt him, but I pushed him. He's dead because of me. Every day for the past nineteen years, that's what I live with. That moment, watching him fall. I don't want that for you."

Malcolm's lips are moving, and his eyes are wide with terror. He knows what's happening to him. And I can't think, I can't.

"I don't want to lose you again," I tell Mom. Salty tears trail down my face and into my mouth.

"Never," she says, inching toward me. "But I'm willing to pay for what I did, and I can't live knowing I'm the reason you took a life."

A sob racks my body as I force the gun to my side.

"Good, baby. Good. Now give it to me."

I let her slip the heavy weight from my fingers.

"There's another phone in the kitchen downstairs." Her lips turn white as she rests the gun on her thigh with her injured arm. She keeps it trained on my grandmother so she can take over for me and hold pressure on Malcolm's wound with her good arm.

She looks like she's seconds from keeling over, but glancing at Malcolm, I realize that just means I'll have to run.

"I can do it," she says, and her word is all I need to push to my feet.

I dash out of the room, skidding into the wall across from the door, my feet momentarily tangling on the rug running the length of the hall. I'm painfully aware of every thudding beat of my heart.

Racing down the stairs, I feel the railing grow warm under my palm from the friction. I leap past the final three steps and start sprinting toward the kitchen. My footsteps echo loudly in the living room. My ears are throbbing, and my ribs are screaming. I don't hear my attacker until arms reach out of the darkness and grab me.

I scream for my mother. It's the only thing I can think to do. A meaty fist swings at my head, but I have so much momentum going that I topple us both forward, slamming us into the island.

There's a butcher block of knives on the counter, and I grab for it with both hands, twisting and smashing it down on his head in the same motion. I catch him right in the temple, and he goes down hard. The smack of his head hitting the stone floor nearly empties my stomach.

The bounty hunter lies motionless, and I'm whirling, jumping at every shadow in the kitchen as my breath whips in and out of me, loud, loud, *loud*. No one else comes at me. I don't know where Blue Eyes is or if he's even here. I yank the phone off the wall so hard it clatters to the floor and skitters up next the bounty hunter, but I don't even hesitate as I dive for it.

9-1-1.

My hand is sweaty, sticky, when I lift the handset to my ear, and I can't think about the red streaks.

Mom's blood.

Malcolm's blood.

Mom's bl—

"Nine-one-one. What is your emergency?"

"Please send help. My mom and my friend have been shot. There's so much blood. Please." I lift my gaze to the ceiling and whisper words that have never hurt so much. "He's dying right now."

"Are you in danger?"

"I—"

The gunshot jolts every bone in my body. I drop the phone and run upstairs.

Run.

Run.

Run.

I fall and run, slip and run. I grab the doorframe and swing myself inside.

The pool of blood beneath Malcolm has stopped growing, Mom is slumped over on her side, and my grandmother lies on the floor with a hole where part of her head should be.

REPAIR

One Year Later

Sometimes just before it's going to rain, when the air grows heavy and the clouds hold their breath, Mom will rub her leg. The wound is long healed, but the ache resurfaces. The one in her shoulder too. No one who meets her now would notice the limp except on the wettest days, but I see it.

It's only when I'm close enough to hug her that the scar tucked up in her hairline is visible. It stretches across her temple and disappears behind her ear. Not that big, considering how much it bled, but they always say scalp wounds bleed the most. I'd say they're right, other than for gunshots to the gut.

When the EMTs arrived that night, I was the one they circled first. We watched the movie *Carrie* on Halloween a few weeks ago, and during the scene when the bucket of blood is dumped on the main character, Mom told me that's what I looked like. None of it was my blood, though.

I'd thought Mom and Malcolm were both dead. They should have been. I'd collapsed between the two of them, burying my face in Mom's bloodied chest and clutching at Malcolm.

But of the four of us left alive that night, I was the one with the most claim to that status.

I had various cuts and bruises, a mild concussion, and a sliced-open forearm, but nothing that kept me in the hospital for long. Not as a patient, at any rate.

Mom and Malcolm didn't fare as well.

Her running days are over, figuratively and literally, and she still has a bullet in her shoulder. It migrated too close to her heart to safely remove.

When I'd screamed out Mom's name downstairs, she'd forgotten about the hole in her shoulder and the gaping wound in her leg. She'd even forgotten about my grandmother. And she tried to army-crawl after me.

My grandmother saw that as her opportunity to grab the eight-inch bronze statue of her late husband off the shelf and try to bash Mom's skull in with it. She got in only one hit before Malcolm, tapping into a reserve of strength the doctors say should have been physically impossible, dragged himself to the gun and shot her.

We still don't know for sure when his ribs broke or whether it was his last-ditch effort to save my mom's life that finally snapped them, but they did puncture his lung, which led to a host of respiratory problems, including a near-fatal bout of double pneumonia. The gunshot did the most damage, though, and he had to endure a number of surgeries to put his insides back together again. He was skeletal and fully bearded when they released him from the hospital, but they did release him. Mom too. And not into police custody either. That was almost more shocking.

Derek Abbott's death was ruled an accident.

Malcolm wasn't arrested for cybercrimes.

And I don't have to live with the burden of having taken a life, since the bounty hunter made a full recovery in time to stand trial for everything he, Blue Eyes, and my grandmother's investigator conspired to do.

We met with various authorities numerous times, but always by choice. I still don't know what handcuffs feel like.

All because of Laura, my father's widow.

And Grace.

It was a big news story when our grandmother died and the manhunt for Derek's accused killer came to an end. Unlike my mother, Laura didn't try to hide the truth from her daughter when she asked. Grace remembered meeting me, and to everyone's surprise, she didn't view me with anything close to animosity. She came to visit me in the hospital to thank me for giving her our great-grandmother's ring.

I cried when she said she made her mother come forward with the truth of what happened the night our father died.

I sobbed when she hugged me.

And I completely broke down when she told me she'd rather have a sister than keep an inheritance all to herself.

She did, though. I've never touched a cent of our grandmother's money.

Our grandmother was buried beside her husband and son. I see her grave whenever Grace and I visit Derek's, but I always keep my distance. Grace is fond of sticking her tongue out at it, but I didn't endure the lifetime of callous cruelty that she did, so I don't feel much of anything when I think of my grandmother. Which I rarely do.

I kept the last name Reed. So did Mom. She did go back to Tiffany, but that didn't change much for us, since I still call her Mom.

I learn more about my father, my birth father, every day. I still don't think of him that way, but Mom gets to, finally.

We also went back to New Jersey. Not to the same house, but near enough that I got to keep my job and I didn't have to change schools. Regina and I are already planning to take graduation photos together in the spring. Mom and I also bring cookies to Mr. Guillory at least once a week, in lieu of paying off the damage done to his car—his request. He's not my actual grandfather, but I find myself pretending sometimes.

Mom has gone to visit her dad a few times now. I can tell how hard it is for her, both because of the deeply damaged relationship they had while she was growing up and because he doesn't remember all the ways he neglected and mistreated her. She's not ready to let me go with her yet, but she promises it will happen one day soon.

These days her promises mean everything.

I also got to see Aiden. It turns out he did interpret my absence as an answer about our relationship and didn't even know anything was wrong until the whole story made the news. We went out a couple more times, and he kept apologizing even though the reality was he couldn't have done anything. In any case, seeing him wasn't the same—few things were—so we ended it. I see him around sometimes, and it makes me miss my old life, if not exactly him.

Malcolm is back in college, and his grandmother is hanging on. We've kept in touch through the occasional email—mostly him giving me advice about which colleges I should consider, since I confessed an extremely late-in-life interest in computers, now that they're no longer off limits to me in any way. There's a veneer of awkwardness to our writing, though. We got to know each other only in the most extreme circumstances, and only for days, at that. I can rarely think of what to say to him, so I end up saying very little.

It'll have to be better in person. I refuse to participate in an anemic conversation once he's standing in front of me. Which he's about to be.

One of the new changes in my relationship with Mom involves her learning to act less like a secret service agent and me learning to make my own decisions. Right now, I'm making the four-hour drive from New Jersey to Penn State to see Malcolm for the first time since he was released from the hospital. Mom probably won't breathe until I'm back home, but I keep telling her to consider it a trial run for when I head to college.

⌐

The little billows of steam have long since faded from my coffee. It wasn't great to begin with, and now that it's cold, every taste on my tongue is an insult.

I keep sipping it, though, no longer disguising the eagerness on my face when the door chimes with the arrival of a new customer to the café.

"You should go freshen that up, hon." A plump woman walking past my table with a sweet smile nods at my mug. She frowns, seeing how little I've drunk, and leans forward. "Who're you waiting for?"

"A friend," I say, twisting to see around her when the door to the coffee shop opens.

"Your friend is pretty late. Sure he's coming?"

I don't answer her. Because suddenly, he's there.

Malcolm.

He's leaner than he used to be, and he kept some of the facial hair, but it's him.

He scans the room, spotting me when I stand, and freezes

in place, half inside, half out. I can tell he's holding his breath, because I'm holding mine.

"Now, that's a look worth waiting for."

I turn to acknowledge the woman with a thank-you, and the moment of indecision breaks. When I turn back, he's walking toward me. Then he's right smack-dab in front of me.

"Hi."

"Hi," I say.

"You kept the bangs."

"Yeah." My hand flies up to make sure the short strands are smoothed down. The scar on my forehead is barely noticeable, but I'm not ready to look at it every day in the mirror and remember.

I don't know which of us ventures a smile first, but the other returns it. I feel the brittleness of my own expression, and I don't know how to ease it. I want to. I want to hug him and grin and laugh, because we're alive and together and not running. But I don't know how to take that step, and every passing second expands the distance between us.

"Do you want some coffee?" I ask, nodding toward the ordering counter. "Or something to eat?"

"Sure."

We both go, because it's better than just standing there. I listen to him place his order. We're side by side. Inches apart. But I felt closer to him when he was out of state. At least then I could pretend.

My jaw is locked, and my heart is a wreck—beating slow, then fast, then somewhere in between. I don't have to be afraid, but I am.

And then I'm not.

Warmth.

Skin.

The back of his hand presses into mine.

ACKNOWLEDGMENTS

I got the idea for *Girl on the Run* at the worst possible time. I was querying agents with what would become my debut novel (*If I Fix You*), and I had just gotten an R&R (revise and resubmit) request from a very respected agent. Every time I tried to work on that R&R, my mind would flood with scenes for this thriller. I tried to ignore them but quickly realized that I had to get the story out of my head and onto the page before I'd be able to think about anything else. I wrote the first hundred pages of what would eventually be called *Girl on the Run* in four days. I literally couldn't type fast enough. Finally able to return to my R&R, I tucked this book aside and went on to land my dream agent with that first book, then sell it and three more books before rereading my thriller and deciding whether those feverish few days of writing had produced anything worth reading.

I thought they had.

249

My agent, Kim Lionetti, and the rest of the amazing team at BookEnds Literary loved it.

And editor extraordinaire Wendy Loggia made me an offer I couldn't refuse.

Kim, I still remember that email you sent after reading those first early chapters. I don't think I've ever smiled harder. Thank you for seeing the potential in Katelyn's story and for working so closely with me to develop the plot. Brainstorming with you is one of my favorite things to do as an author.

I'm so grateful to my editors, Wendy Loggia and Audrey Ingerson, and the entire team at Underlined and Penguin Random House for taking this book and making it so much more than I could have dreamed.

Sarah Guillory and Kate Goodwin, can you believe this is an actual book? Thank you for your endless encouragement and the many, many times you both read early drafts. You make everything I write so much better, and I would not have become published without you. Thank you also to Rebecca Rode for always being ready to lend your truly talented eye to anything I send your way. I'm so glad that PitchWars brought us together.

I'm also indebted to the AZ YA/MG group for surrounding me with talented and inspiring authors: Kelly DeVos, Kate Watson, Amy Trueblood, Amy Dominy, Nate Evans, Dusti Bowling, Joanna Ruth Meyer, Stephanie Elliot, Sara Fujimura, Kara McDowell, Traci Avalos, Karen Chow Hsu, Tom Leveen,

Paul Mosier, Lorri Philips, Glynka FritzMiller, Riki Cleveland, Shonna Slayton, Mallory Suzanne, and so many more!

To my parents, Gary and Suzanne Johnson, thank you for instilling in me a love for action movies from a young age, especially Bruce Willis and Arnold Schwarzenegger movies. To my siblings, Sam, Mary, and Rachel, thanks for reenacting totally unsafe action scenes with me when we were kids—and when we weren't really kids anymore and should have known better. Ross and Jill, cofounders of House Balls and that super-dangerous game that involved jumping off the balcony onto mattresses . . . thanks for marrying my siblings and growing our family in the best way possible. To Ken Johnson, Nate Williams, Rick & Jeri Crawford, and the Depews, I love you all. To my nieces and nephews—Grady, Rory, Sadie, Gideon, Ainsley, Ivy, Dexter, Os, and Goldie—being your aunt is the best part of my life.

READ ANOTHER PAGE-TURNING
THRILLER FROM UNDERLINED.

TURN THE PAGE FOR AN EXCERPT.

CHAPTER 1

TO: 9781579126247@gmail.com

SUBJECT: The Game Begins

I am ready to kill or be killed. This email serves as the official notice that I, [NAME HERE], am entering this year's round of Assassins. I understand that I must send this email before midnight Wednesday and that I will receive the rules, my team members' names, and my target's name Friday at 12:00 p.m.

The game begins Friday at 5:00 p.m.

Wish me luck,

[NAME HERE]

"This is it," Lia said. She added her name to the email and read it over one last time. "Think we'll be the first?"

"I didn't wake up at five to not be." Gem launched themselves off the bathroom counter and peered over Lia's shoulder. "It's simpler than I thought it would be."

"Dramatic, though." Lia nudged Gem in the side. "Do yours. We'll send them together."

Every March, in the anxiety-ridden weeks before colleges sent out acceptance decisions, the seniors of Lincoln High went to war. The game was the last great equalizer before the seniors went their separate ways.

And Lia—who had been planning her Assassins strategy since ninth grade, who had color-coded it red in her planner, and who had never been the best at anything—had already hung on her closet door a practical pair of running shoes, a black T-shirt she only mostly cared about, and a pair of leggings that wouldn't feel like sandpaper if they got wet.

Not that they would. She just liked to be prepared.

"Gem Hastings reporting for murder." Gem took a step back and raised their phone.

This year, the invitation to play was taped to the back of the bathroom doors. Few teachers ever ventured into these bathrooms, and even if one did, every bathroom was the same. Powder soap dusted the damp counters and inspirational posters decorated the dented stall doors. The invitation was a large poster of the white Lincoln High lion overlaid with three concentric circles in blood red. At their center was a QR code.

Assassins wasn't a school-approved event, but it was tradition. Anyone who wanted to play would know what this poster meant.

"Scanned," Gem said. The email opened, and they filled it out. "Three."

"Two," Lia said, thumb hovering over the SEND button.

It was only a game, but it was *the* game. It was hunting season for seniors. It was permission to stay out late with friends and teammates. It was the last chance for Lia to be good at something instead of being stuck in the shadow of her older brother.

"One," they both said.

The emails sent.

"I hope we're on the same team," Lia said, "or else we had better get used to murdering each other."

Gem snorted. "Should I not have already gotten used to that?"

Lia and Gem had been best friends since third grade—after an incident with the school-issued square pizza and May Barnard's face—and had been inseparable ever since, even though Gem's loathing for May had shifted to a crush this last year.

"Look at us!" Gem spun Lia to the mirror and rested their chin atop her head. "We're going to win."

A crack in the mirror split Lia's long face in half and made her green eyes uneven. Behind her, Gem's tall, muscled form was split and squished.

Their phones dinged with the same message:

Hello, Lia Prince & Gem Hastings.
Welcome to the game and happy hunting.
The Council

"Think this means we're on the same team?" Gem asked.

"Maybe." Lia shook her head, rubbed the back of her neck, and picked up her backpack. "It means that whoever the Council is knows us well enough to assume we're together right now."

"You know," Gem said, turning away, "even if we don't win, it'll be a good way to spend time together before next year."

"We'll win." Lia shook her head at her shattered image in the mirror. Gem won lots of things—best grades, theater tournaments, and test score competitions. The only award Lia had ever gotten was for attendance. "I just wish the Council told us everything up front."

No one knew who the Council was or how they were chosen, but the rumor was that it was three seniors handpicked by the previous year's Council. Everyone in Lincoln knew each other and their deepest secrets, so Lia had always assumed that rumor was true. The town was too small to keep such a mystery for so long.

"I bet it's Gabo," Gem said. "He loves stuff like this."

Gabriel Gutierrez, math genius and theater nerd, was one of Lia's guesses for the Council, too. His older brother had won Assassins seven years ago and had given him all his old notes. Gabriel even had a hand-me-down tricked-out water gun.

Mark, Lia's older brother, had placed third but had never told her anything helpful.

"Don't worry," Lia said. "The Council always teams up friends, families, and crushes to keep the real fighting to a minimum."

In the years before the Council became anonymous and focused more on the teammate and target assignments, friendships had been ruined and relationships dashed due to Assassins.

"I hope we get May as a target," Gem said as they joined the crush of students in the hall.

Seniors opened bathroom doors and tugged their friends inside. Lia kept an eye on the ones who vanished inside for only a minute, noting their names or descriptions. There were 317 seniors, and Lia had spent all last year figuring out who would play. She had been left with fifty definites.

She had documented their daily schedules and which classrooms they were in this semester. Her journal was filled to the edges with names, maps, and by-the-minute timetables. Lia clutched it to her chest and wound her way upstairs to the biology lab with Gem.

Gem opened the door. "Stalking everyone?"

Lia waved her journal. "Not everyone, and it's all stuff they say aloud. It's not like I'm following them home. Stalking makes it sound weird and illegal."

Once the game was on and Lia had her first target, she would be following them home, but even she knew that sounded creepy.

A student snorted behind Lia, and she turned. Faith Franklin was frowning at her, her eyes going from Lia's muddy shoes to the soda-stained journal in her hands.

"Not illegal, Prince," Faith said. She was always immaculate from her pin-straight brown hair to her pure white tennis shoes. "Definitely weird, though."

Lia hadn't bothered documenting Faith; the girl hated games as much as she hated mess. Faith sat at the first bench in the biology lab and pulled out a bullet journal bursting with stickers and notes. Hannah, who sat behind her, pulled out some new calligraphy pen to show her. Lia dropped her journal and half-chewed pen onto a bench next to Gem.

"She's so organized," Lia said. "I bet her closet is gorgeous."

"Don't worry." Gem pulled out their work and grinned. "Once we win the game, nothing will be able to hold us back. We'll be unrivaled."

Lia laughed. "I don't think they give scholarships out for fake-murdering classmates."

In class, Lia had always been very, very rivaled.

With AP exams looming and their fates soon to arrive in admission portals, everyone took to the lab with as much liveliness as the day-old sheep eyeballs they were dissecting. At the next table, Devon Diaz, Lia's oblivious crush since seventh grade, was the only one really following the steps of the lab and not just cutting the eye into tiny pieces. His fingers curled around the handle of his scalpel as if it were his violin bow, steady and sure of every move. He blew his black hair, a touch too long and curling at the ends, out of his eyes and rolled his shoulders back. Devon was sharper than any note he ever played, always wearing button-down shirts and dark jeans. He was put together and knew exactly what he wanted—all A's, pre-med, and no distractions. Like dating.

Specifically, like dating Lia.

Near the end of class, Gem leaned over and whispered, "If Devon's our target, will you be able to kill him?"

"Of course I could kill him," Lia said, already calculating how hard she would have to pull the trigger to let loose the least amount of water. "But he's not playing."

"Did you ask him?" Gem asked. "You never talk to him."

"Yes."

This was a lie. Lia hadn't asked him. She'd just watched him for months. They moved in similar but distant circles, and he liked talking about music and how math touched everything. Lia could listen to him talk for hours, and sometimes did when she happened upon him talking to someone else and she could listen from the other side of a corner or bookshelf. He had no interest in what she could talk about—escape rooms, games, and sometimes art—but he was always kind enough to listen to her anyway. He would nod and smile, nudging her to keep talking. He was too nice.

And he always laughed at her jokes no matter how goofy they were.

"I never thought you'd have the nerve," Gem whispered.

Lia held up the small Nerf pistol—accuracy over deluge—she had started carrying in her bag Monday to get used to the weight. She didn't want any surprises come Friday. She sprayed Gem once, only lightly on the shoe, and a few drops of water splattered across the floor. Abby looked up from the book in her lap across the aisle.

Lia shrugged and mouthed, "Sorry."

Abby covered her laughter with the book as Ms. Christie gathered their worksheets and took them across the hall to the classroom.

"I could hear you talking about me, you know," Devon said, turning around. He spun his scalpel across his knuckles like a pen. "If I was playing, I would take you out first."